文法封神榜

Uncover the Hidden Power

武董 ◎ 著

第一本神話英文文法故事書！

見證「千古傳奇」、體會「人間有情」
發掘自我潛能，立即脫胎換骨，
重拾你遺忘許久的英文文法

三大學習架構

- 封神榜故事 ▶ 全書中英對照，由耳熟能詳的故事，例如姜太公遇文王、比干的七竅玲瓏心等，「聽」、「讀」並用，雙管齊下學文法。
- 文法正誤句 ▶ 透過正誤句解析，釐清文法概念，不再傻傻分不清楚！
- 文法出題要點 ▶ 釐清**120**個文法重點，並搭配文法關鍵知識學習，最後參照文法解析充分理解文法內容。

MP3

作者序
Author

　　這本書是為初、中級英文學習者企劃編寫的文法學習書。藉由古典神話故事「封神榜」中的內容，編撰出三十五個故事單元。讀者可以在重溫古典文學作品的同時進階英文能力。

　　本書的每個單元都依照故事情節拆分為兩個小單元，再以正誤句和出題要點的模式分別做文法解析。其中文法正誤句整理了諸多常見的文法出錯點，透過對正誤例句的解析釐清文法概念；文法出題要點則採用英文考試中多項選擇題的方式，融合了解題技巧和文法考點的分析，協助讀者即效性學習。本書介紹的文法點大部分是初級文法，間中融入少量中級文法，對英文略有基礎的讀者而言，是一本相對簡單的創新式文法學習書。希望這本書對您的英文學習有所裨益。

武董

目 次
Contents

🌊 **Unit 01**│周文王 – 連接詞、條件句

　　1-1 封神榜小故事 會飛的老虎...........................008

　　1-2 封神榜小故事 為父母所遺棄.....................011

🌊 **Unit 02**│周文王 – 副詞連接詞、慣用語

　　2-1 封神榜小故事 軒轅殿大火.........................016

　　2-2 封神榜小故事 女媧廟參拜.........................019

🌊 **Unit 03**│伯逸考 – 慣用語、連接詞

　　3-1 封神榜小故事 伯逸考之死 024

　　3-2 封神榜小故事 伯逸考靈魂化身成兔子 028

🌊 **Unit 02**│周文王 – 慣用語、副詞

　　4-1 封神榜小故事 文王聘姜尚 032

　　4-2 封神榜小故事 渭水河畔遇文王 036

🌊 **Unit 05**│哪吒 – 連接詞、慣用語

　　5-1 封神榜小故事 哪吒割肉還母、剔骨還父 040

　　5-2 封神榜小故事 哪吒廟 044

Unit 06｜哪吒 – 慣用語、使役動詞、關係代名詞

　　6-1 封神榜小故事 哪吒復活.......................048

　　6-2 封神榜小故事 父子關係惡化.......................052

Unit 07｜妲己 – 動詞、慣用語

　　7-1 封神榜小故事 妲己設計酷刑 056

　　7-2 封神榜小故事 炮烙 059

Unit 08｜雷震子問世 – 慣用語

　　8-1 封神榜小故事 雷震子問世.......................064

　　8-2 封神榜小故事 黃金雷錘.......................068

Unit 09｜比干 – 慣用語

　　9-1 封神榜小故事 比干除妖.......................072

　　9-2 封神榜小故事 狐狸皮衣.......................076

Unit 10｜比干 – 慣用語、副詞連接詞

　　10-1 封神榜小故事 七竅玲瓏心 080

　　10-2 封神榜小故事 無心菜 084

Unit 11｜黃飛虎 – 關係代名詞、同位語

　　11-1 封神榜小故事 黃飛虎投奔西岐 088

　　11-2 封神榜小故事 黃飛虎遭擒 092

Unit 12｜哪吒 – 名詞、指示代名詞、副詞連接詞

　　12-1 封神榜小故事 哪吒大戰張桂芳 096

　　12-2 封神榜小故事 哪吒打敗張桂芳.......................099

Unit 13｜姜子牙 – 慣用語、動詞、條件句

　　13-1 封神榜小故事 姜子牙險失封神榜 104

13-2 封神榜小故事 打賭......................108

🌀 **Unit 14 | 姜子牙 –** 關係代名詞、被動語態

14-1 封神榜小故事 姜子牙收徒龍鬚虎 112

14-2 封神榜小故事

姜子牙戰勝了九龍島大師們.....................116

🌀 **Unit 15 | 聞太師 –** 時態、情緒動詞

15-1 封神榜小故事 破解十絕陣 120

15-2 封神榜小故事 異常凶險 123

🌀 **Unit 16 | 楊戩 –** 名詞、所有格、慣用語

16-1 封神榜小故事 二郎神楊戩 128

16-2 封神榜小故事 卓越的能力 131

🌀 **Unit 17 | 姜子牙戰勝趙公明 –** 慣用語

17-1 封神榜小故事 姜子牙戰勝趙公明 136

17-2 封神榜小故事 巫術.......................140

🌀 **Unit 18 | 鄧九公 –** 被動、時態、慣用語

18-1 封神榜小故事 鄧九公出征 144

18-2 封神榜小故事 遁地術.....................148

🌀 **Unit 19 | 土行孫 –** 關係代名詞、不定詞、動詞

19-1 封神榜小故事 收服土行孫 152

19-2 封神榜小故事 懼留孫.....................156

🌀 **Unit 20 | 鄧九公 –** 時態、慣用語

20-1 封神榜小故事 蘇護討伐西岐................160

20-2 封神榜小故事 鄧九公的背叛.................164

Unit 21｜楊戩 – 名詞、時態、定冠詞

21-1 封神榜小故事 西岐瘟疫 168

21-2 封神榜小故事 尋求解藥 172

Unit 22｜殷洪 – 慣用語、名詞子句、副詞連接詞

22-1 封神榜小故事 殷洪的宿命 176

22-2 封神榜小故事 慈航道人帶來了一幅地圖..180

Unit 23｜殷郊的背叛 – 慣用語、條件句、複數名詞

23-1 封神榜小故事 殷郊的背叛 184

23-2 封神榜小故事 四面旗子 188

Unit 24｜姜子牙 – 慣用語、不定詞、副詞

24-1 封神榜小故事 孔雀製造的麻煩 192

24-2 封神榜小故事 準提馴服了孔雀 195

Unit 25｜通天教主 – 分詞、時態

25-1 封神榜小故事 通天教主被激怒 200

25-2 封神榜小故事 懼留孫制服了申公豹 204

Unit 26｜楊戩 – 名詞、動名詞、條件句

26-1 封神榜小故事 化血神刀的解藥 208

26-2 封神榜小故事 三粒解藥 211

Unit 27｜余元 – 被動語態、慣用語、形容詞

27-1 封神榜小故事 余元殞命 216

27-2 封神榜小故事 余元被輾為兩半 219

Unit 28｜四位道人 – 關係代名詞、情態動詞、被動語態

28-1 封神榜小故事 誅仙陣前的較量 224

28-2 封神榜小故事 摧毀誅仙陣 228

Unit 29｜姜子牙 – 時態、關係代名詞、慣用語

29-1 封神榜小故事 姜子牙連破三關.................232

29-2 封神榜小故事 神焰扇毀瘟癀陣.................235

Unit 30｜元始天尊 – 慣用語、動詞

30-1 封神榜小故事 破萬仙陣.................240

30-2 封神榜小故事 所有計劃都被粉碎了.........244

Unit 31｜紂王 – 時態、主動詞一致

31-1 封神榜小故事

武王吉兆降臨，紂王末日狂歡.................248

31-2 封神榜小故事 對紂王失去信念.................261

Unit 32｜千里眼和順風耳 – 動詞、時態、關係副詞

32-1 封神榜小故事 千里眼和順風耳.................256

32-2 封神榜小故事 摧毀兩精靈.........................260

Unit 33｜楊戩 – 慣用語、形容詞

33-1 封神榜小故事 楊戩打敗梅山七怪............264

33-2 封神榜小故事 女媧娘娘之助.....................267

Unit 34｜紂王 – 時態、限定詞、名詞子句

34-1 封神榜小故事 剷除昏君.................272

34-2 封神榜小故事 商朝的結束.................276

Unit 35｜姜子牙 – 被動語態、分詞

35-1 封神榜小故事 姜子牙封神.................280

35-2 封神榜小故事 眾神之神.................284

周文王

連接詞、條件句

1-1 封神榜小故事 | 🎧 *MP3 01*
會飛的老虎

The Flying Tiger

Ji Chang (姬昌) the Western Lord, later becoming the Wen Wang (文王) of Zhou Dynasty, is one of the main protagonists in the traditional mythology novel <The Apotheosis of Heroes>. Wen Wang is an expert in deviation and future prediction; he once speculated Nezha's (哪吒) destiny. Nezha's father Li Jing (李靖) is renowned as the most prominent commander officer in late Shang Dynasty; Nezha is the youngest son among Li Jing's three boys. Nezha is very special as his mother Lady Yin (殷十娘) experienced three years and six months pregnancy before finally giving birth to him.

When Nezha was born, he appeared as a ball of flesh. Li Jing hit the ball with a sword as he misapprehended the ball as a monster. Then a three-year-old Nezha jumped out from the ball and surprised everyone.

會飛的老虎

傳統神話小説《封神演義》的主角之一西伯侯姬昌，也就是後來的周文王，非常擅長卜卦和預測未來。他曾經預測出哪吒的命運。哪吒的父親李靖是商朝末年的名將。哪吒是李靖的三個兒子中年紀最小的，他非常特別，是母親殷十娘懷胎三年六個月才生出來的。哪吒出生的樣子是一顆肉球，被李靖誤以為是妖怪而揮劍劈開，三歲的哪吒就從球中蹦出來，令眾人大吃一驚。

文法正誤句

KEY 1

Ji Chang is <u>one of the main protagonists</u> in the traditional mythology novel <The Apotheosis of Heroes>.

Ji Chang is <u>one of the main protagonist</u> in the traditional mythology novel <The Apotheosis of Heroes>.

姬昌是傳統神話小說《封神演義》中的主角之一。

解析 one of … 後需要接名詞複數，表示……之一。在這個句子中，「眾多主角」應當為複數 protagonists。

⟲ KEY 2

○ He once speculated Nezha's (哪吒) destiny.

✗ He was used to speculate Nezha's (哪吒) destiny.

中譯 他曾預測出哪吒的命運。

解析 once 指曾經，當副詞時有曾經的意思；而 be used to 表示對某件事感到習慣，或習以為常，後接名詞或動名詞，如 I am used to it，但在語意上是不對的。

⟲ KEY 3

○ When Nezha was born, he appeared as a ball of flesh.

✗ When Nezha was born, he appeared as a meatball.

中譯 哪吒出生的樣子是一顆肉球。

解析 此處形容哪吒出生的樣貌，而 meatball 是專指食物肉丸子。

KEY 4

○ Li Jing hit the ball with sword as he misapprehended the ball as a monster.

✗ Li Jing hit the ball with sword <u>as of</u> he misapprehended the ball as a monster.

中譯 李靖誤以為是妖怪而揮劍劈開了那顆球。

解析 As 用作連接詞其後可以接表示原因的子句；而片語 as of 後面接的則是時間點，表示從這個時間開始或截至這個時間為止，如：as of today。

1-2 封神榜小故事 | 🎧 MP3 02
為父母所遺棄

Abandoned by parents

Wen Wang met Nezha and foretold his future. <u>He notified Nezha's mother Lady Yin that this boy would experience catastrophic calamities in his future life. Unless Nezha is fortunate enough to meet a 'flying tiger', the crisis will not be resolved.</u> As expected, the antemortem King of Shang had a dream that when Nezha grows up, this boy would become the one who destroys Shang Dynasty. The King implored his faithful commander Li Jing to kill Nezha for the future of the nation. Li Jing made up his mind that he would sacrifice his own son, but was faced with a strong opposition by lady Yin. The couple made a compromise and abandoned Nezha at the Flying Tiger Mountain Creek letting the gods decide Nezha's fate.

<u>After being abandoned by his parents, Nezha felt desperate and helpless. Luckily, a general named Huang Feihu (黃飛虎), the name literally means the 'flying tiger', passed by and saved Nezha.</u> Huang Feihu adopted Nezha and raised him as his own son. With the help of the 'flying tiger', Nezha managed to grow up smoothly.

周文王見到哪吒後預見了他的未來，他告知哪吒的母親殷十娘此子將來會遭遇大劫難，除非他遇到一隻會飛的老虎，否則無法化險為夷。果然不久後，商朝皇帝在臨死前夢見哪吒將來長大後會對商朝不利，懇請忠臣李靖殺死哪吒。李靖下了決定，要犧牲他的兒子，忠於主君，這遭到殷十娘的竭力反對。夫婦倆最後決定將哪吒遺棄在飛虎澗聽天由命。

哪吒被父母遺棄後，感到極為絕望無助。幸運的是一位叫做「黃飛虎」的將軍，他的名字正好是「會飛的老虎」的意思，剛好路過那裡並救下哪吒。黃飛虎收養了哪吒，並把他當作自己的小孩疼愛，在「飛虎」的幫助下，哪吒才得以順利地長大。

「文法出題要點」

（　）1. He notified Nezha's mother Lady Yin _____ this boy would experience catastrophic calamities in his future life.

（A）that　　　（B）this　　　（C）they　　　（D）it

答　案	A
題目中譯	他告知哪吒的母親殷十娘告知此子將來會遭遇大劫難。
文法重點	名詞子句的連接詞。
關鍵知識	空格前後分別是完整結構的句子，需要連接詞。That 是引導名詞子句的可以省略的連接詞。
文法解析	四個選項裡只有 that 可以做為子句連接詞使用。That 既可做主句動詞的受詞，也可以做主句主詞的補充說明。其餘三個字則只有普通代詞功能。

（　）2. _____ Nezha is fortunate enough to meet a 'flying tiger', the crisis will not be resolved.

（A）Unless　　　　　　（B）if Only
（C）Not only　　　　　（D）When only

A

哪吒只有遇到一隻會飛的老虎，才有可能化險為夷。

Only if (unless) 與 if only 的用法及區別

Only if 後接限制性條件句。If only 則表示說話人對某事寄予厚望。

Only if 的意義是「只有……才……」，後接的子句是主句得以達成的必要條件。If only 則是加強語氣的 if，常用在虛擬語氣中表達遺憾或願望，意思是「要是……就太好了」，如 If only he could come，但願他能來。在這個題目中，哪吒只有遇見會飛的老虎，命運才有轉機，應當是用 only if。C 要與 but also 搭配使用，D 則是錯誤用法。

(　) 3. After＿＿＿＿＿ by his parents, Nezha felt desperate and helpless.

(A) abandoned　　　　　(B) be abandoned
(C) being abandoned　　(D) abandoning

C

哪吒被父母遺棄後，感到極為絕望無助。

被動語態和介詞＋動名詞。

主詞是動詞的接受方，要用被動語態。

文法解析　After 在此處是介詞，其後必須接名詞或動名詞，而不可以接動詞原形，因而只有 C 和 D 符合文法規則。而哪吒是被遺棄，因而要用 being abandoned。

（　）4. Luckily, a general named Huang Feihu, the name literally means the 'flying tiger', passed by and ＿＿＿＿＿＿ Nezha.

（A）saved
（B）saving
（C）have saved
（D）had saved

答　　案　A

題目中譯　幸運的是一位叫做「黃飛虎」的將軍，剛好路過那裡並救下哪吒。

文法重點　對等連接詞前後的動詞時態要一致。

關鍵知識　And 連結的兩個字彙應當是相同時態，不應當出現過去式 and 現在式，或現在式 and 將來式的混搭狀況。

文法解析　路過和解救是主詞黃飛虎同時做出的動作，因而時態應當一致。Passed by 用了一般過去式；與之對應，saved 也是一般過去式。

周文王

副詞連接詞、慣用語

2-1 封神榜小故事 | 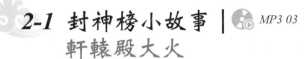 MP3 03
軒轅殿大火

Great Fire in Conflagration in Xuanyuan Hall (軒轅殿)

Wen Wang also had successfully predicted the destiny of the Shang Dynasty. At the end of Shang Empire, Zhou Wang (紂王) inherited the crown. Zhou Wang indulged his passion in debauchery after his accession to the throne. He never showed any interest in the state management, which made many faithful ministers including Ji Chang anxious about the new king's behavior; they constantly expostulated with Zhou Wang on paying more attention to the national affairs. However, Zhou Wang ignored people's suggestions.

Zhou Wang selected beautiful girls from all over the country and gathered them in the palace. Su Hu (蘇護), the minister in Jizhou, was discontent with Zhou Wang's tyranny. <u>He dispatched troops to rebel against Zhou Wang, but was defeated by the troops of Zhou.</u> To apologize for his offence, Su Hu had to send his daughter Su Daji (蘇妲己) to Zhou Wang.

 ## 軒轅殿大火

周文土也曾成功預測了商朝的國運。商朝末年，紂王繼位。紂王繼位後沈迷於酒色，終日不理朝政。包括姬昌在內，許多忠誠的大臣，都對新君主的行為感到非常焦慮。他們不斷諫言紂王要更用心經營國家。只是紂王完全不理會大家的建議。

紂王遴選天下美女入宮，冀州侯蘇護不滿紂王暴虐荒淫，起兵反抗商帝國，但被紂王的軍隊打敗。為了謝罪，蘇護只得將女兒蘇妲己獻給紂王。

 ## 文法正誤句

 ### KEY 5

 Zhou Wang indulged his passion in <u>debauchery</u> after his accession to the throne.

✗ Zhou Wang indulged his passion in <u>debauched</u> after his accession to the throne.

中譯 紂王繼位後沈迷於酒色。

解析 名詞 debauchery 表示墮落，縱情於酒色；而同字根的 debouched 是形容詞，表示放蕩的，墮落的，此處介詞 in 後面應當是一個名詞。

KEY 6

○ Many honest ministers <u>including</u> Ji Chang became anxious about the new king's behavior.

✗ Many honest ministers <u>included</u> Ji Chang became anxious about the new king's behavior.

中譯 包括姬昌在內，許多忠誠的大臣，都對新君主的行為感到非常著急。

解析 動詞 include 的現在分詞 including 和過去分詞 included，都可以在句子中做介詞使用，和名詞／代詞一起組成片語，意思是包括……在內。固定的搭配方法是 including＋名詞，以及名詞＋included。

KEY 7

○ They constantly <u>expostulated with Zhou Wang on paying</u> more attention to the national affairs.

✗ They constantly <u>expostulated Zhou Wang pay</u> more attention to the national affairs.

中譯 他們不斷諫言紂王要更用心經營國家。

解析 不及物動詞 expostulate 有勸導、忠告、諫言的意思，固定的用法搭配為 expostulate with sb on/about……。

KEY 8

○ He dispatched troops to rebel against Zhou Wang, but <u>was defeated</u> by the troops of Zhou.

✗ He dispatched troops to rebel against Zhou Wang, but <u>defeated</u> by the troops of Zhou.

中譯 他起兵反抗商帝國，但被紂王的軍隊打敗。

解析 主詞 hc 是動詞 defeat 的承受者，因而要用被動語態。

2-2 封神榜小故事│ 🎧 *MP3 04*
女媧廟參拜

A visit to the Nuwa (女媧) Shrine

<u>Once, Zhou Wang made a formal visit to the Nuwa (女媧) Shrine.</u> He was so astonished by the beauty of Nuwa's statue that he fell in love with her at first sight. Zhou Wang even wrote a poem with the hope of marrying the

goddess. Nuwa was furious at Zhou Wang's irreverence. She sent the Fox Witch to make troubles in Zhou Wang's palace, expecting that it would accelerate the extinction of the Shang Dynasty. The fox made itself living inside Su Daji's body and got ready to instigate disasters to Zhou Wang.

Zhou Wang was extremely happy about Daji's arrival; however, Ji Chang forecasted this beautiful girl would destroy the dynasty. Ji Chang persuaded Zhou Wang into killing Daji but the king shut his eye to the suggestion. Ji Chang then proclaimed that his prediction would be proven by a big fire in the Xuanyuan Hall at night. The king was extremely cautious and prohibited everyone from lighting up torches. Nonetheless, there was still a fire during that very night. This incident had made people believe in Ji Chang's prediction.

 女媧廟參拜

一次，紂王去女媧宮參拜。他驚豔於看到女媧娘娘聖像的美貌，對她一見鍾情，甚至寫詩希望迎娶女媧為妻。女媧大怒之下派出狐狸精去宮廷搗亂，以期加速商朝的滅亡。狐狸精附身在蘇妲己身上，準備在紂王身邊造成禍患。

　　妲己入宮令紂王十分高興，但姬昌預測出美麗的妲己會毀滅商朝。他向紂王建議除掉妲己，紂王置之不理。姬昌於是預言當晚軒轅殿將會發生火災以證明自己的預測。紂王十分小心，命令所有人當晚都不准點火。但是那一晚軒轅殿還是起火了，此事令人們相信了姬昌的預言。

「文法出題要點」

（　）1. Once, Zhou Wang _____ a formal visit to the Nuwa Shrine.

　　（A）make　　　　　　（B）made
　　（C）makes　　　　　（D）have made

答　　案	B
題目中譯	一次，紂王去女媧宮參拜。
文法重點	時態的運用。
關鍵知識	描述過去發生的事情用一般過去式。
文法解析	Once 表示時間的副詞，標明是一件曾經發生的事，動詞應當用 made。

（　）2. Zhou Wang was extremely happy about Daji's arrival; _____, Ji Chang forecasted this beautiful girl would destroy the dynasty.

（A）otherwise （B）however

（C）besides （D）hence

答　案　B

題目中譯　妲己入宮令紂王十分高興，但姬昌預測出美麗的妲己會毀滅商朝。

文法重點　副詞連接詞連接兩個對等的句子。

關鍵知識　使用副詞連接詞時，以分號；和逗點，放在副詞連接詞前後，以連接兩個分句。

文法解析　按照前後兩個分句的意義，判斷選用哪一個副詞連接詞。Otherwise 指其他方面，有選擇的意味；however 表示轉折；besides 是此外、而且的意思；hence 表示因此，解釋原因。此處的轉折連接詞應當是轉移意味的 however。

（　）3. The king was extremely cautious and prohibited everyone _____ lighting up torches.

（A）from （B）by （C）to （D）for

答　案　A

題目中譯　紂王十分小心，命令所有人當晚都不准點火。

文法重點 　動詞和介詞的固定搭配。

關鍵知識 　阻止某人做某事是 prevent sb from doing sth。

文法解析 　表示阻止的動詞 ban，prevent 和 prohibit 的用法都是後面直接接 sth 或 sb from doing sth。

（ 　）4. This incident had made people ＿＿＿＿＿ in Ji Chang's prediction.

（A）believe

（B）to believe

（C）believing

（D）believed

答　案 　A

題目中譯 　此事令人們相信了姬昌的預言。

文法重點 　使役動詞用法。

關鍵知識 　Make sb do sth 是固定用法

文法解析 　Make、have、let 是三個使役動詞，後面接省略 to 的不定式做受詞補語，因而固定的形式為 make/have/let sb do sth，應當選擇動詞原形。

伯逸考

慣用語、連接詞

3-1 封神榜小故事 | *MP3 05*
伯逸考之死

The death of Boyikao (伯逸考)

Boyikao is Wen Wang's oldest and most preeminent son. Ji Chang possessed outstanding ability as well as moral excellence, which made Zhou Wang worry that one day he would betray him. Hence, Zhou Wang imprisoned Ji Chang in the capital of Shang. Boyikao who loved his father so much, felt miserable for Ji Chang's prisoned life. Boyikao took several treasures to the capital, and pleaded with Zhou Wang to release his father and accept himself as the hostage.

Daji fell in love with handsome Boyikao at first sight.

By means of instrument learning, she was able to approach Boyikao very often, but her favor was turned down by Boyikao. Her feelings for Boyikao went from love to hatred. <u>She suggested that Zhou Wang kill Boyikao and make his flesh into meatballs</u>, and then presented them to Ji Chang. If Ji Chang eats the meatballs; it can be proven that his ability to predict was merely bluffing, and he had nothing to be afraid of.

伯逸考之死

　　伯逸考是文王的長子，並且是文王最優秀的兒子。姬昌的能力和德行都極為優秀，這導致商紂王擔心他有朝一日會背叛自己，於是將姬昌囚禁在商的首都。伯逸考非常孝順，不忍心父親被監禁。他帶著寶物來找紂王求情，希望自己可以代替父親作人質。

　　妲己看到伯逸考英俊倜儻，對他一見傾心。她藉著學琴名義頻繁接近伯逸考，但她的愛慕之情遭到了伯逸考的嚴詞拒絕。妲己由愛生恨，向紂王建議殺掉伯逸考並把他做成肉丸，拿給姬昌吃。如果姬昌吃下肉丸，就證明他所謂的預言能力根本就是被吹噓出來的，完全不足為懼。

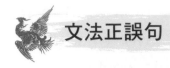

文法正誤句

KEY 9

○ Boyikao is Wen Wang's oldest and most preeminent son.

✕ Boyikao is Wen Wang's oldest and most preeminent sons.

中譯 伯逸考是文王的長子,並且是文王最優秀的兒子。

解析 主詞是單數名詞伯逸考,動詞為 is,所以介系詞表語為單數名詞 son,而非 sons。

KEY 10

○ Ji Chang possessed outstanding ability as well as moral excellence; which made Zhou Wang worry that one day he would betray him.

✕ Ji Chang possessed outstanding ability as well as moral excellence; made Zhou Wang worry that one day he would betray him.

中譯 姬昌的能力和德行都極為優秀,這導致商紂王擔心他有朝一日會背叛自己。

解析　由 wihch 引導的形容詞子句修飾前面的主句。在子句中，
which 是做主詞不能省略。

🔥 *KEY 11*

○ By means of instrument learning, she was able to
approach Boyikao very often.

✕ By instrument learning, she was able to approach
Boyikao very often.

中譯　她藉著學琴名義頻繁接近伯逸考

解析　By means of 表示以……憑藉，根據句子的意義，學琴可
以做接近人的藉口，琴本身不可以。

🔥 *KEY 12*

○ She suggested that Zhou Wang kill Boyikao and
make his flesh into meatballs.

✕ She suggested that Zhou Wang kill Boyikao and
made his flesh into meatballs.

中譯　她向紂王建議殺掉伯逸考並把他做成肉丸。

解析　Kill 和 make 都是妲己建議紂王做的事，收到 suggest to
的限制，都要用動詞原形。

伯逸考靈魂化身成兔子

Boyikao's spirit incarnates into rabbits

Ji Chang found out the death of his beloved son from divinatory symbols. However, he received the meatball breakfast sent from Zhou Wang the next morning. Ji Chang knew that the king had set this trap to test him; so he pretended that he knew nothing about it, forcing himself to eat the breakfast with great sorrow. Finally, Zhou Wang was reassured that Wen Wang had no superpowers. He felt relieved and set Wen Wang free.

Ji Chang experienced severe nauseousness as soon as he arrived at the land of Zhou. He vomited out three little rabbits, which were the embodiment of Boyikao's spirits. Boyikao was the first victim in the fight against Zhou Wang. After he passed away, his soul reached the Heavenly Southern Gate, the Lord of Venus set him into the purple myrtle constellation and made him divine.

姬昌由卦象得知了愛子已經被害，第二天卻收到了紂王特地派人送來的肉丸早餐。姬昌知道紂王設置了這個圈套來測試他，所以裝作一無所知，強忍痛苦吃下了早餐。最終紂王放心相信文王不具有超能

力，他顧慮全失，釋放了文王。

　　姬昌一踏上周的土地就感到強烈的噁心。他嘔出了三隻小白兔，那是伯逸考的魂魄所化成的兔子。伯逸考是對抗紂王的第一個犧牲者，他死後魂魄來到南天門，太白金星將他安在紫微星宮，成為了尊貴的神。

 「文法出題要點」

（　）1. Ji Chang found out the death of his ＿＿＿＿ son from divinatory symbols.

　　（A）beloved 　　　　（B）loved
　　（C）love 　　　　　（D）loving

答　　案　　A
題目中譯　　姬昌由卦象得知了愛子已經被害。
文法重點　　修飾名詞的形容詞。
關鍵知識　　Beloved 表示親愛的、摯愛的，beloved son/daughter 是愛子／愛女的固定用法。
文法解析　　形容詞 beloved 意思是摯愛的；loved 做形容詞時表示戀愛的；love 是名詞／動詞，不能修飾名詞；loving 做形容詞表示忠誠的，鍾情的，和句子意思不符合。

（　）2. Ji Chang knew that the king _____ this trap to test him.

　　（A）had set　　　　　（B）set
　　（C）have set　　　　 （D）sets

答　案　A

題目中譯　姬昌知道紂王設置了這個圈套來測試他。

文法重點　動詞時態。

關鍵知識　主句影響從屬子句的時態。

文法解析　姬昌已知一個事實，是已經發生的事情，要用完成式；
　　　　　而主句本身是過去式，因而子句時態為過去完成式。

（　）3. Finally Zhou Wang was reassured _____ Wen Wang had no superpowers.

　　（A）whom　　　　　（B）when
　　（C）which　　　　　（D）that

答　案　D

題目中譯　最終紂王放心相信文王不具有超能力。

文法重點　名詞子句的連接詞。

關鍵知識　wh～、how、that 都可以做名詞子句的連接詞。

文法解析　That 引導的名詞子句做主句的受詞，這種用法時 that 不具有特別的意義，而且可以省略。其餘的連接詞都有各自的含義，不能用在此處。

（　）4. Ji Chang experienced severe nauseousness _____ he arrived the land of Zhou.

（A）as well as　　　　（B）as quickly as
（C）as long as　　　　（D）as soon as

答　案　D

題目中譯　姬昌一踏上周的土地就感到強烈的噁心。

文法重點　as...as...的用法。

關鍵知識　As adj/adv as 表示和……一樣。

文法解析　As well as 表示不但……而且……；固定用法 as quickly as possible 表示儘快地；as long as 表示只要……，既然……；as soon as 表示一……就……。因而 D 符合句子的意義。

周文王

慣用語、副詞

4-1 封神榜小故事 | 🎧 *MP3 07*
文王聘姜尚

Jiang Shang (姜尚) recruited by Wen Wang

Jiang Tai Gong (姜太公) has a courtesy name Ziya (子牙), and a Dharma name Flying Bear. He is Wen Wang's best assistant, and also the most privileged strategist as well as military commander in the Zhou dynasty. Before meeting Jiang Ziya, Wen Wang once dreamt about a tiger with wings rampaging towards him. Wen Wang was shocked by the dream; he consulted some erudite ministers about the meaning of this dream, getting pretty good feedback that it actually meant something propitious. It forecasted that one day, a sage would appear to help him, and the state would become prosperous.

Jiang Ziya used to serve Zhou Wang for many years, but he could not tolerate the way Zhou Wang treated people. <u>He feigned madness and escaped from the capital.</u> Jiang Ziya believed his expertise in military affairs must be useful somewhere else. He then waited placidly for a wise king to show up.

姜太公字子牙，道號飛熊。他是周文王的得力助手，也是西周地位最高的謀士和統帥。周文王遇見姜子牙之前，曾經夢到一隻長著翅膀的猛虎向他飛撲過來。文王被這個夢嚇醒，他向博學的大臣們請教這夢的意義。文王得到了好的答案：這是一個吉夢，它預示了今後將有智者出現來輔佐文王，國家會變得興旺。

姜子牙曾為紂王服務多年，他無法容忍紂王對待人民的方式，就裝瘋逃出了都城。姜子牙相信自己的軍事才能一定有用武之地，於是他就靜待明君的出現。

  文法正誤句

 **KEY 13**

Before meeting Jiang Ziya, Wen Wang once <u>dreamt about</u> a tiger with wings <u>rampaging</u> towards him.

✗ Before meeting Jiang Ziya, Wen Wang once <u>dreamt to</u> a tiger with wings <u>rampage</u> towards him.

中譯 周文王遇見姜子牙之前，曾經夢到一隻長著翅膀的猛虎向他飛撲過來。

解析 Dream 是名詞夢，或動詞作夢。Dream 的過去式和過去分詞可以有兩種變化，分別是 dreamt 和 dreamed。類似的動詞還有 lean, learn, spell, burn, leap, light, smell 等，都是有兩種過去式和過去分詞。Dream 用作動詞的固定搭配是 dream of 或 dream about ＋ 名詞／動名詞。容易犯的錯誤則是 dream to＋原形動詞。

KEY 14

○ He <u>consulted some erudite ministers</u> about the meaning of this dream.

✗ He <u>consulted</u> about the meaning of this dream.

中譯 他向博學的大臣們請教這夢的意義。

解析 Consult 表示尋求意見或訊息時是一個及物動詞，後面應當有名詞做受詞。

KEY 15

○ It forecasted that one day, a sage would appear to help him, and the state would become prosperous.

✗ It forecasted that one day, a sage will appear to help him, and the state will become prosperous.

中譯 它預示了今後將有智者出現來輔佐文王，國家會變得興旺。

解析 It forecasted 是過去式，後面的子句為 forecast 的內容，用過去未來時，would／should＋原形動詞。

KEY 16

○ He feigned madness and escaped from the capital.

✗ He feigned madness and escape from the capital.

中譯 他發瘋逃出了都城。

解析 由 and 連起來的兩個動詞彼此是並列關係，時態應當一致。

Encounter with Wen Wang at the Wei River

The way Jiang Ziya acted during his exile time was quite unique. He fished in a tributary of the Wei River, using a straight and barbless hook, and the hook was hung three meters over the water. Everyone passing by was confused for his way of fishing; Jiang Ziya explained: when time is ready, the fish would come to him by their own volition. Wen Wang performed divination and realized that an important person would show up at the Wei River. He devoutly followed rules to purify himself for the meeting before heading to the Wei River. When Wen Wang encountered Jiang Ziya, who sat on a grass mat fishing, he immediately realized this unusual white-haired fisherman was the person he really needed. They had a conversation on statecraft and Wen Wang appointed Jiang Ziya as the prime minister. After Wen Wang died, his son Wu Wang inherited the throne and Jiang Ziya assisted Wu Wang to overthrow the Shang Dynasty.

渭水河畔遇文王

　　姜子牙隱居時期的行為非常特別，他在渭水的支流垂釣，用無餌的直鉤，且魚鉤還距離水面三尺。每個路過的人都對他的釣魚方式感到困惑，姜太公解釋道：時機成熟的時候，魚兒會主動來找他。文王卜卦後發現有個重要的人物會出現在渭水河畔，在去渭水之前，文王虔敬地遵守禮儀淨化自己。當文王遇見坐在草蓆上釣魚的姜子牙時，他馬上就意識到這個不尋常的白髮漁翁就是他真正需要的人。他們談論了治國理念，文王聘請姜子牙為丞相。文王過世後，他的兒子武王繼位，武王在姜子牙的輔佐下推翻了商朝。

「文法出題要點」

（　）1. He fished in a tributary of the Wei River, ＿＿＿ a straight and barbless hook, and the hook was hung one meters over the water.

（A）uses　　　　　　（B）used

（C）use　　　　　　（D）using

答　　案　D

題目中譯　他在渭水的支流垂釣，用無餌的直鉤，且魚鉤距離水面三尺。

文法重點　時態的運用。

分詞引導的副詞子句修飾主句動詞。

文法解析 用無餌魚鉤這一狀態修飾了前面句子的動詞 fished。

分詞可以引導副詞子句，如果分詞的動作是主句的主詞
發出的，則使用現在分詞；如果主句主詞是分詞動作的
接受者，則用過去分詞。

( ) 2. Everyone passing by ＿＿＿＿＿＿ confused for his way of fishing.

（A）was　　（B）were　　（C）is　　（D）are

答　案　A

題目中譯　每個路過的人都對他的釣魚方式感到困惑。

文法重點　單複數與時態。

關鍵知識　Every 後面的名詞要使用單數型態。

文法解析　Every 和 each 修飾的名詞都是第三人稱單數；由於
句子是過去時態，動詞要選用過去式。

( ) 3. He devoutly followed rules to purify himself for the meeting before ＿＿＿＿＿＿ to the Wei River.

（A）go　　　　　　　　（B）heading

（C）went （D）gone

答　　案	B
題目中譯	在去渭水之前，文王虔敬地遵守禮儀淨化自己。
文法重點	介系詞片語。
關鍵知識	After, before, when 等從屬連接詞，假若主句跟子句主詞相同，就可以把主詞省略掉，後面動詞改為分詞。
文法解析	這裡的 before 也是介系詞，before heading to…成了介系詞片語。 而介系詞之後只能接現在分詞。

（　）4. They had a conversation on statecraft and Wen Wang ＿＿＿＿＿＿ Jiang Ziya the prime minister.

（A）invited （B）invite
（C）appointed （D）appoints

答　　案	C
題目中譯	他們談論了治國理念，文王聘請姜子牙為丞相。
文法重點	動詞的選擇。
關鍵知識	invite sb to do sth 和 appoint sb sth。
文法解析	appoint 用作委任某人某職位是 appoint sb sth。 invite 邀請、邀約一般的用法是邀請某人做某事 invite sb to do sth。

Unit 05

哪吒

連接詞、慣用語

5-1 封神榜小故事 | MP3 09
哪吒割肉還母、剔骨還父

Nezha returns body to his parents／
哪吒割肉還母、剔骨還父

Nezha is mischievous, lively, and quite emulative. When Nezha was seven years old, he once played by the sea with other children. His treasures stimulated the sea and caused a tsunami; even the dragon palace down in deep ocean was shaken by the wave. The Eastern Sea Dragon King was angry and sent his third son to check on what had happened. Nezha had a fierce fight with the Dragon Prince, who was eventually slain by Nezha.

The Dragon King was furious for his son's death. He

confronted Nezha's family and threatened to flood the whole country for a revenge. To save his family and all the innocent people, Nezha decided to commit suicide. Nezha carved his own body and dismembered his bones, then returned his flesh and bones to his parents. The Dragon King was pleased to find out about Nezha's death and stopped punishing Nezha's family.

哪吒割肉還母、剔骨還父

　　哪吒個性活潑頑皮，且爭強好勝。他七歲時，和幾個同伴在在海邊玩。哪吒身上的寶物將海水攪動起來引發了海嘯，連海底的龍宮也因之震動。東海龍王非常生氣，派三太子去看個究竟。龍王三太子和哪吒大打出手，三太子最後被哪吒殺死。

　　三太子的死激怒了龍王，龍王找到哪吒的家人，威脅要令全國河水氾濫作為報復。為了救家人和無辜的百姓，哪吒決定自殺賠罪。哪吒分解了自己的肉身和骨頭，將它們還給了父母親。龍王對哪吒的死表示滿意，停止懲罰哪吒全家。

文法正誤句

KEY 17

○ Nezha is mischievous, lively, and quite emulative.

✗ Nezha is mischievous, lively and quite emulative.

中譯 哪吒個性活潑頑皮,且爭強好勝。

解析 如果 and 連接三個以上的字或片語,除了最後那個在 and 之後的字,其他的後面都要加逗點。

KEY 18

○ His treasures stimulated the sea and caused a tsunami; even the dragon palace down in deep ocean was shaken by the wave.

✗ His treasures stimulated the sea and caused a tsunami; even the dragon palace down in deep ocean was shook by the wave.

中譯 哪吒身上的寶物將海水攪動起來引發了海嘯,連海底的龍宮也因之震動起來。

解析 Shake 的過去式為 shook,過去分詞是 shaken,此處的被動態應當用過去分詞。

KEY 19

The Eastern Sea Dragon King was angry and <u>sent his third son to check</u> on what had happened.

The Eastern Sea Dragon King was angry and <u>sent his third son checking</u> on what had happened.

中譯 東海龍王非常生氣，派三太子去看個究竟。

解析 Send sb to do sth 意思是讓某人去做某事，do sth 是目的；send sb doing sth 是讓某人開始做某事，強調 doing的動作，譬如 the punch sent him running downstairs，一拳令他向樓下衝去。

KEY 20

The Dragon King was pleased to find out about Nezha's death and <u>stopped punishing</u> Nezha's family.

The Dragon King was pleased to find out about Nezha's death and <u>stopped to punish</u> Nezha's family.

中譯 龍王對哪吒的死表示滿意，停止懲罰哪吒全家。

解析 Stop doing 是指停止做某事，即 doing 這個動作不再繼續了；stop to do 是指停下本來正在做的事，開始 to do 的這個動作。故應當是 stop doing。

Nezha Temple

After Nezha passed away, his soul had left the body. One night, Lady Yin had a dream. In the dream, Nezha told his mother that his soul was seeking for somewhere to rest. He asked Lady Yin to build a temple for him.

Lady Yin believed Nezha had never left, and the dream was a message from him, so she secretly built a temple for Nezha. Soon afterwards, this temple flourished. People admired the spirit of the little hero and sick people could always grant miraculous recoveries after visiting Nezha's temple. Nezha's temple was extremely well known and only his father Li Jing was kept in the dark. Li Jing was firmly convinced that Nezha was an ominous trouble maker; his death was a release and all the family members should cut off connections with Nezha. Hence, Lady Yin deliberately hid the information of Nezha's temple from her husband.

哪吒廟

哪吒過世之後，他的靈魂離開了身體。一天晚上，殷十娘做了一個夢。在夢裡哪吒對母親說他的魂魄要找一個地方安放。他請殷十娘為自己造一座廟。

殷十娘相信哪吒並沒有真的離開，這個夢境就是他傳來的訊息。所以她悄悄為哪吒建了一座廟。不久之後，哪吒廟變得香火鼎盛。人們都敬重小英雄的精神，而且生病的人去哪吒廟拜謁後常常都能得到奇蹟地好轉。哪吒廟人盡皆知，只有他父親李靖被蒙在鼓裡。李靖深信哪吒是一個災星，他的死終於讓家人得以解脫，所有人必須要切斷和哪吒的關聯。所以殷十娘故意向李靖隱瞞了哪吒廟的存在。

「文法出題要點」

（　　）1. In the dream Nezha told his mother _____ his soul was seeking for somewhere to rest.

（A）while　　　　　（B）this

（C）which　　　　　（D）that

答　案　D

題目中譯　在夢裡哪吒對母親說他的魂魄要找一個地方安放。

文法重點　That 做連接詞。

由連接詞 that 引導的子句主要都是介紹言論或思想，有時 that 可以省略掉。

此處空缺的並不是關係子句中的關係代名詞，而是接在動詞後面的連接詞，只有 that 有這種文法功能。

（　）2. Soon afterwards, this temple _____.

（A）flourished　　　　　（B）multiplied
（C）increased　　　　　（D）escalated

A

不久之後，哪吒廟變得香火鼎盛。

動詞的選擇。

表示繁榮、進步、增加的字。

依據上下文的意義，廟宇變得更有人氣應當選用 flourish；multiply, increase 和 escalate 都不能確切描述廟宇的狀態。

（　）3. Nezha's temple was _____ well known and only his father Li Jing was kept in the dark.

（A）so　　　　　　　（B）extremely
（C）too　　　　　　　（D）such

答　　案	B
題目中譯	哪吒廟人盡皆知，只有他父親李靖被蒙在鼓裡。
文法重點	副詞的選擇。
關鍵知識	So, too, such 在句子裡形容程度，常有固定用法 so...that..., too…to…, such…that。
文法解析	so...that..., too…to…, such…that 表示太……以致於……，如此地……以致於……；在這個句子中缺少與 so, too, such 相匹配的後半部分，只有 extremely 適用。

（　）4. Hence, Lady Yin deliberately hid the information on Nezha's temple ＿＿＿＿＿＿ her husband.

（A）towards （B）with 　　（C）from 　　（D）for

答　　案	C
題目中譯	所以殷十娘故意向李靖隱瞞了哪吒廟的存在。
文法重點	介系詞的選擇。
關鍵知識	可以用 hide sth from sb, prevent sth from being known, keep sth secret 來表示隱瞞的意思。
文法解析	表示隱藏、隱蔽、隱瞞時常用介系詞 from，與動詞 hide, conceal 等搭配。

哪吒

慣用語、使役動詞、關係代名詞

6-1 封神榜小故事 | 🔘 MP3 11
哪吒復活

The reincarnation of Nezha

Three years after Nezha's temple was built, Li Jing came across it. He dropped in to make a wish only to find that it was Nezha's temple. Li Jing thought the temple was another trick of Nezha's, a trick that would lead to more troubles. So he angrily destroyed Nezha's statue and burnt the temple down.

The Master of the Clouds (雲中子) once told Nezha if he spends three years on quiet introspection, he will reincarnate into a human. But all his efforts were shattered by Li Jing's destruction. Nezha's soul flew to his master Taiyi Immortal (太乙真人), who used lotus roots to construct a human body and lotus leafs to make clothes. Nezha was brought back to life this way.

哪吒復活

哪吒廟建好三年後，李靖偶然經過。他進去許願，發現原來是哪吒廟。李靖覺得這座廟又是哪吒的花招，會引來更多的麻煩。所以他憤怒地砸毀哪吒的雕像並燒毀了哪吒廟。

雲中子曾經告訴哪吒，如果他用三年時間靜心反省，就可以重新轉世為人。可是哪吒所有的努力都被李靖粉碎了。哪吒的魂魄飛到了他的師父太乙真人那裡，太乙真人以蓮藕為肉、荷葉為衣，重造了哪吒，令他得以復活。

文法正誤句

KEY 21

○ Three years after Nezha's temple was built, Li Jing came across it.

✗ Three years after Nezha's temple was built, Li Jing came across.

中譯 哪吒廟建好三年後，李靖偶然經過。

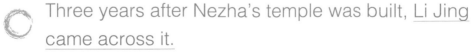

解析 Come across 和 come over 做及物動詞時，意思是偶然發現、偶然遇到，後面需要接 somebody／something。Come across 做不及物動詞時，有呈現方式的意思，或對某種人或物的特定看法，例如：It depends on how well you come across in the presentation. She comes across as very confident.

KEY 22

○ He dropped in to make a wish only to find that it was Nezha's temple.

✗ He dropped into make a wish only to find that was Nezha's temple.

中譯 他進去許願，發現原來是哪吒廟。

解析 Drop in／drop by／drop round 都有短暫訪問的意思，drop in to make a wish 是兩個連續發生的動作，而 drop into 只有掉進去的意思，後面要接一個名詞。

KEY 23

○ The Master of the Clouds once told Nezha if he spends three years on quiet introspection, he will reincarnate into a human.

The Master of the Clouds once told Nezha <u>if he could spend three years</u> on quiet introspection, <u>he would</u> reincarnate into a human.

中譯 雲中子曾經告訴哪吒，如果他用三年時間靜心反省，就可以重新轉世為人。

解析 這個句子是 if 引導的條件句。在假設的狀況有可能發生時，主句是一般將來時，條件子句的動詞用一般現在式。錯誤例句中用了 would，一般用在描述與現實相反的虛擬語氣中。

KEY 24

Nezha's soul flew to his <u>master Taiyi Immortal, who used</u> lotus roots to construct a human body and lotus leafs to make clothes.

Nezha's soul flew to his <u>master Taiyi Immortal, whom used</u> lotus roots to construct a human body and lotus leafs to make clothes.

中譯 哪吒的魂魄飛到了他的師父太乙真人那裡，太乙真人以蓮藕為肉、荷葉為衣，重造了哪吒。

解析 關係代名詞主格銜接動詞，太乙真人做出製造哪吒的動作，應當用主格 who 而非受格 whom。

A worsening relationship between father and son

Taiyi Immortal gave Nezha two new weapons: the Wind Fire Wheels (風火輪) and the Fire-tipped Spear (火尖槍). Not only that, Nezha still possessed his Universe Ring (乾坤圈) and the Red Armillary Sash (渾天). These weapons made Nezha more powerful.

Burning the temple had worsened Li Jing's relationship with Nezha. They had fought several times after Nezha's reincarnation and Li Jing can no longer defeat Nezha. Nezha insisted to claim his farther's life which forced Li Jing to commit suicide. Wenshu Guangfa Tianzun (文殊廣法天尊) saved Li Jing's life, educating Nezha that he should submit to his father. To restrain Nezha from rebelling further, the deity Master Burning Lamp gave Li Jing a pagoda, so whenever he is about to rebel, Li Jing can trap Nezha inside it. Thus, the enmity between father and son was relieved; Li Jing and Nezha later could cooperate with each other in Wu Wang's troop.

父子關係惡化

太乙真人送給哪吒兩件新武器：風火輪和火尖槍。不但如此，哪吒還擁有他的乾坤圈和渾天 。這些武器令哪吒更加強大。

燒毀哪吒廟使得李靖和哪吒的關係更加惡化。哪吒復活後兩人已經惡戰幾次，而李靖再也無法打敗哪吒。哪吒堅持要殺死父親，這使得李靖被逼自殺。文殊廣法天尊救了李靖性命，他教育哪吒應當順從父親。為了約束哪吒的反叛行為，仙燃燈道人給了李靖一座寶塔，今後哪吒不服從父親時就可以將他收在塔裡。這樣，父子間的敵意得以緩解。李靖和哪吒後來在武王麾下相互合作。

「文法出題要點」

（　）1. Those weapons made Nezha more ＿＿＿＿＿.

　（A）capability　　　　（B）capacity

　（C）powerful　　　　（D）power

答　　案　C

題目中譯　這些武器令哪吒更加強大。

文法重點　動詞 make 的用法。

關鍵知識　Make 做使役動詞時，後面接原形動詞 make sb do sth。另一種用法 make sb adj，這裡受詞 sb 後接

形容詞做受詞補語。

Capability, capacity 和 power 都是名詞，只有 powerful 是形容詞，符合此處的文法需求。

(　) 2. Burning the temple ＿＿＿＿＿＿＿ his relationship with Nezha.

（A）had worsen 　　　　（B）had worsened
（C）had worse 　　　　　（D）worse

答　　案　　**B**

題目中譯　燒毀哪吒廟使得李靖和哪吒的關係更加惡化。

文法重點　動詞的選擇。

關鍵知識　及物動詞 worsen 表示變得更糟、使惡化，由形容詞 worse 變化而來。

文法解析　過去完成式 had 後面接過去分詞，worsen 的過去分詞為 worsned。

(　) 3. Nezha insisted to claim his farther's life; this forced Li Jing ＿＿＿＿＿＿ suicide.

（A）commit 　　　　　　（B）to commit
（C）committing 　　　　（D）committed

| 答　案 | B |

題目中譯　哪吒堅持要殺死父親，這使得李靖被逼自殺。

文法重點　使役動詞 force 的用法

關鍵知識　Force 與一般的使役動詞不同，不說 force sb do sth，而是 force sb to do sth。

文法解析　強迫某人做某事的慣用法是 force sb to do sth，不可以直接接動詞原形或分詞形式。

（　）4. To _____ Nezha from rebelling further, the deity Master Burning Lamp gave Li Jing a pagoda, so whenever he is about to rebel, Li Jing can trap Nezha inside it.

（A）restrain　　　　　（B）restrained
（C）restraining　　　　（D）will restrain

答　案　A

題目中譯　為了約束哪吒將來的反叛行為，仙燃燈道人給了李靖一座寶塔，今後哪吒不服從父親時就可以將他收在塔裡。

文法重點　不定詞 to+V。

關鍵知識　不定詞後加原形動詞，表目的。

文法解析　不定詞後加原形動詞所以須用原形動詞 refrain，refrain…from 為固定用法表示為了…約束。

Unit 07

妲己

動詞、慣用語

7-1 封神榜小故事 *MP3 13*

妲己設計酷刑

A cruel torture designed by Daji／妲己設計酷刑

　　Zhou Wang was extremely infatuated with Daji. He spent all his time with Daji and spared no effort to please her. Master of the Clouds from the Zhongnan Moutain (終南山) found out the capital city was in a sinister atmosphere, so he took a legend sword to the palace. Master of the Clouds told Zhou Wang that there must be some evil spirits in the palace. Hanging the sword in the palace center would suppress the monster from making troubles.

Daji fell seriously sick after the sword had been hung up. Zhou Wang felt heartbroken seeing Daji suffering from illness, so he burnt the sword down at Daji's request. Soon after that Daji had recovered. At the same time, Master of the Clouds disappointedly found that the sinister atmosphere surrounding the capital had become even thicker.

妲己設計酷刑

紂王對妲己非常著迷，他花所有時間和妲己在一起，不遺餘力的取悅她。終南山的雲中子看到都城裡妖氣迷漫，就攜帶一把仙劍來到了宮中。雲中子告訴紂王宮裡必定有妖孽，把仙劍掛在皇宮正中央有望壓制住妖怪的作亂。

仙劍掛好之後妲己就大病一場。紂王看到妲己生病心痛不已，他在妲己的要求下燒掉了仙劍。不久後妲己就痊癒了。與此同時，雲中子失望地發現都城的妖氣變得更重。

文法正誤句

KEY 25

○ Zhou Wang <u>was extremely infatuated</u> with Daji.

✗ Zhou Wang extremely <u>infatuated</u> Daji.

紂王對妲己非常沈迷。

解析 Infatuate 做動詞是使沈迷的意思，慣常用法是 be infatuated with sb/sth.

🔥 KEY 26

⭕ Hanging the sword in the palace center would suppress the monster from making trouble.

❌ Hanged the sword in the palace center would suppress the monster from making trouble.

中譯 把仙劍掛在皇宮正中央有望壓制住妖怪作亂。

解析 過去分詞沒有名詞的作用，不能在句子裡做主詞和受詞。只有現在分詞即動名詞才有名詞的性質。

🔥 KEY 27

⭕ Daji fell seriously sick after the sword had been hung up.

❌ Daji fell seriously sick after the sword had been hanged up.

中譯 仙劍掛好之後妲己就大病一場。

解析 動詞 hang 懸掛的過去式和過去分詞都是 hung。唯一的例外情況是表示用絞刑將人處死時，過去式和過去分詞為 hanged。

KEY 28

At the same time, Master of the Clouds disappointedly found that the <u>sinister atmosphere surrounding the capital had become</u> even thicker.

At the same time, Master of the Clouds disappointedly found that the <u>sinister atmosphere surrounding the capital becomes</u> even thicker.

中譯 與此同時，雲中子失望地發現都城的妖氣變得更加瀰漫。

解析 依時態須用過去完成式，故用 had become thicker，都城的妖氣是變壞的。

7-2 封神榜小故事｜ MP3 14
炮烙

Paolo

To satisfy her taste of collecting rare species, Daji built her own zoo in the palace. <u>Zhou Wang sent hundreds of soldiers to hunt birds and beasts in the hopes of ingratiating her.</u> Daji also loved lustful music and dancing. <u>She forced maids in the palace to perform nude dancing; those who protested the performance were executed by Zhou Wang.</u>

Several ministers reminded Zhou Wang to be aware

of devils close by. Daji was very angry; she told Zhou Wang these rumour spreaders must be severely punished. She invented a method of torment called Paolo (炮烙). A bronze cylinder was heated to an extremely hot temperature; then the victim was forced to walk barefoot on top of the furnace. Whenever the victim loses his balance, he will drop into fire and be burnt to death. Zhou Wang used Paolo to torture and kill those who oppose him; and Daji enjoyed watching people suffering from this torture. Everyone felt frightened. As a result, no one dared to remind Zhou Wang of focusing on state affairs anymore.

炮烙

　　妲己在宮中建了動物園，以滿足她收藏珍稀物種的愛好。為了討好妲己，紂王派出幾百名士兵去捕捉珍禽異獸。妲己還很喜愛淫穢的音樂和舞蹈。她強迫宮女們裸體表演舞蹈，拒絕表演的人都被紂王處死。

　　幾位大臣提醒紂王要小心身邊的妖怪。妲己非常生氣，告訴紂王一定要嚴懲這些散播謠言的人。她設計了一種叫作炮烙的刑罰：把銅柱燒得滾燙，強迫受害人光腳走在爐火上。當受害人失去平衡，就會掉進火中被燒死。紂王用炮烙之刑折磨死反對他的人；妲己則在觀賞人們受刑時獲得樂趣。所有人都感到非常恐懼，結果再也沒有人提醒紂王要勤政了。

「文法出題要點」

（ ） 1. Zhou Wang sent hundreds of soldiers to hunt _____ in the hopes of ingratiating her.

  （A） birds and animals
  （B） beauty and beast
  （C） birds and beasts
  （D） birds and cockatoo

答　案　C

題目中譯　為了討好妲己，紂王派出幾百名士兵去捕捉珍禽異獸。

文法重點　and 連接兩個性質一致的字。

關鍵知識　前文提到妲己的愛好是蒐集 rare species，選擇與 species 對應的選項。

文法解析　鳥和動物，鳥和鸚鵡都不是對等的關係，只有 birds and beasts 是合適的選項。

（ ） 2. She forced maids in the palace to perform nude dancing; _____ who protested the performance were executed by Zhou Wang.

  （A） these　　　　　　（B） those
  （C） this　　　　　　（D） that

答 案	B
題目中譯	她強迫宮女們裸體表演舞蹈，拒絕表演的人都被紂王處死。
文法重點	Those who 的用法。
關鍵知識	Those 是先行詞，those 後面省略名詞 people；who 是關係代詞。
文法解析	Those who 是 those people who 的省略形式，表示 whoever, anyone，凡是……的人。

( ) 3. whenever the victim loses his balance, he will drop into fire and _____ to death.

（A）burnt　　　　　　（B）burn

（C）burns　　　　　　（D）be burnt

答 案	D
題目中譯	當受害人失去平衡，就會掉進火中被燒死。
文法重點	動詞的時態。
關鍵知識	時間副詞子句提出先決條件，主句則為結果。
文法解析	將會掉入火中並且被燒死，被火燒是被動語態，要用 be burnt。

（　）4. Daji enjoyed _____ people suffering form this torture.

（A）watch　　　　　　　（B）to watch

（C）watching　　　　　（D）watches

答　　案	C
題目中譯	妲己在觀賞人們受刑時獲得樂趣。
文法重點	Enjoy 的用法。
關鍵知識	及物動詞 enjoy 後面要接受詞，如果受詞是動詞，須改為動名詞。
文法解析	Enjoy doing 是固定用法。Enjoy 後面不能直接接動詞，也不可以是 enjoy to do。

Unit 08

雷震子

慣用語

8-1 封神榜小故事 | MP3 15
雷震子問世

The birth of Leizhenzi

Once, Ji Chang and his troops were walking in a mountain. Suddenly a thunderstorm came, but after the rain, bright sunshine astonished everybody. Ji Chang said a golden light following a thunderbolt is a sign of creating a celestial angel. The next moment, Ji Chang's subordinate commander found an abandoned baby in a temple near by. Ji Chang adopted this baby as his son. He named the boy Leizhenzi. Among Ji Chang's one hundred adopted sons, Leizhenzi was the only immortal one. Master of the Clouds knew that this baby was destined to assist Ji Chang in the creation of a new dynasty; he took Leizhenzi as his disciple and educated him with superb skills.

Even as a kid, Leizhenzi was strong and muscular. He learnt from Master of the Clouds at Zhongnan Mountain for several years. When Leizhenzi turned seven, Master of the Clouds sent him to a cliff. Leizhenzi found two large red apricots at the edge of the cliff. After Leizhenzi ate the apricots, his face turned blue, his hair turned red, and two wide wings sprouted from his back.

 ## 雷震子問世

　　有一次，姬昌帶兵走往山裡。突然電閃雷鳴，下起大雨，但不久之後又雨過天晴，耀眼的陽光讓所有人為之驚嘆。緊接著，姬昌感嘆雷電之後的金光是創造天使的象徵。接著姬昌手下的將軍就從附近的廟裡找到一個棄嬰。姬昌把這個嬰兒收做自己的養子，給孩子取名為「雷震子」。在姬昌的一百個養子中，雷震子是唯一的神仙。雲中子知道這個嬰孩注定要協助姬昌建立新的王朝，他收雷震子為徒弟，傳授他絕技。

　　即使還是個小孩，雷震子就已經力大無窮。他追隨雲中子在終南山修行多年。雷震子七歲的時候，雲中子讓他去爬一處懸崖。雷震子在懸崖邊發現兩顆大紅杏，雷震子把紅杏吃下後，臉變成藍色，頭髮變成紅色，背後也生出一對翅膀。

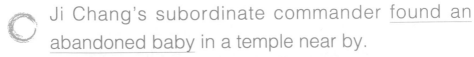

文法正誤句

KEY 29

○ Ji Chang's subordinate commander <u>found an abandoned baby</u> in a temple near by.

✗ Ji Chang's subordinate commander <u>found out an abandoned baby</u> in a temple near by.

中譯 姬昌手下的將軍從附近的廟裡找到一個棄嬰。

解析 Find 主要指偶然發現或者透過尋找而發現某人／某物；find out 主要表示通過調查弄清楚了事情的真相。

KEY 30

○ Master of the Clouds knew that this baby <u>was destined to assist</u> Ji Chang in the creation of a new dynasty.

✗ Master of the Clouds knew that this baby <u>was destined assisting</u> Ji Chang in the creation of a new dynasty.

中譯 雲中子知道這個嬰孩注定要協助姬昌建立新的王朝。

解析 註定的慣用法是 be destined to，不是接動詞 ing 形式。

KEY 31

When Leizhenzi turned seven, Master of the Clouds sent him to a cliff.

When Leizhenzi turned seven, Master of the Clouds sent him a cliff.

中譯 雷震子七歲的時候,雲中子讓他去爬一處懸崖。

解析 用 send 時,表示「指派某人做某事」為 send sb to do sth;若表示「使得某人做某事」則用 send sb doing sth,有被動的意味此處為 send him to a cliff,錯誤句中少了 to。

KEY 32

After Leizhenzi ate the apricots, his face turned blue, his hair turned red, and two wide wings sprouted from his back.

After Leizhenzi ate the apricots, his face turns blue, his hair turns red, and two wide wings sprouted from his back.

中譯 雷震子把紅杏吃下後臉變成藍色,頭髮變成紅色,背後也生出一對翅膀。

解析 主句和表時間的副詞子句的時態應當都是過去式。

Golden Thunder Rod (黃金雷錘)

With the wings, Leizhenzi could not only fly, but also produce wind and thunder by flapping the wings. Master of the Clouds gave him the Golden Thunder Rod (黃金雷錘) as his weapon and instructed him to support his father whenever needed.

When Ji Chang was chased by Zhou Wang's soldiers, Leizhenzi arrived in time. Zhou Wang's people were shocked by Leizhenzi's appearance, and were too timid to challenge monster-looking Leizhenzi. Leizhenzi flew into the sky and created a rockslide with his Golden Thunder Rod, which scared all the soldiers away. Leizhenzi asked Ji Chang to sit on his back. They flew across five mountains until finally reaching the safe place. At his departure, Leizhenzi promised Ji Chang that he would practise diligently in Zhongnan Mountain and would serve Xiqi one day.

黃金雷錘

有了雙翅後，雷震子不僅可以飛，還可以拍動翅膀製造風雷。雲中子給他黃金雷錘作為武器，並指導雷震子在義父需要幫助時出手搭救。

當姬昌被紂王的人追殺時，雷震子及時趕到。紂王的士兵被雷震子的相貌震懾住，都不敢挑戰長得像妖怪的雷震子。雷震子飛到空中，用黃金雷錘將山岩劈落，這把士兵們都嚇跑了。雷震子讓姬昌坐在他背上，他們飛過五座大山直到抵達安全的地方。他在告別時向姬昌承諾，自己會在終南山努力修習，有朝一日為西岐效力。

「文法出題要點」

（　）1. Leizhenzi could not only _____ , but also produce wind and thunder by flapping the wings.

　　（A）fly　　　　（B）flying　　（C）flies　　　（D）flew

答　案	A
題目中譯	雷震子不僅可以飛，還可以拍動翅膀製造風雷。
文法重點	Not only … but also 的用法。
關鍵知識	Not only … but also 是對等連接詞，意思是不但……而且……，所連接的單字須用相同的詞性。

fly 和 produce 都要用原形動詞，因為這兩個詞都收到情態動詞 could 的修飾。

( ) 2. When Ji Chang was chased by Zhou Wang's soldiers, Leizhenzi arrived _____.

　　（A）at all times　　　（B）at times
　　（C）on time　　　　　（D）in time

答　　案　　D

題目中譯　　當姬昌被紂王的人追殺時，雷震子及時趕到。

文法重點　　與 times 有關的片語。

關鍵知識　　In time 是及時的意思，而 on time 是準時的意思。

文法解析　　On time 有已經設置好時間表，準點到達的意思；at times 表示偶爾，at all times 表示時時刻刻、始終。此處應當為 in time。

( ) 3. Leizhenzi flew into the sky and created a rockslide with his Golden Thunder Rod; which _____ all the soldiers away.

　　（A）required　　　　（B）stimulated
　　（C）forced　　　　　（D）scared

答 案	D
題目中譯	雷震子飛到空中，用黃金雷錘將山岩劈落，這把士兵們都嚇跑了。
文法重點	依據上下文選擇合適的動詞。
關鍵知識	雷震子劈落山岩的舉動應當是令人害怕，所以動詞應選擇與害怕相關的。
文法解析	需要、激勵、強迫在此處都不是貼切句意的動詞，嚇跑比較準確。

（   ）4. They flew _____ five mountains until finally reached the safe place.

（A）high　　　　　　（B）above

（C）across　　　　　（D）away

答 案	C
題目中譯	他們飛過五座大山直到抵達安全的地方。
文法重點	Across 的用法。
關鍵知識	Across 表示橫越，從一邊到達另一邊。
文法解析	Fly away 表示飛走，above 和 high 也無法表現雷震子背著義父飛越大山的狀態。

Unit 09 比干

慣用語

9-1 封神榜小故事 MP3 17
比干除妖

Bigan (比干) eliminated bogeys／比干除妖

After Ji Chang returned to Xiqi, he experienced a tremendous increase in prestige. Jiang Ziya's help also made Xiqi a more prosperous kingdom. Zhou Wang's uncle Bigan realized the potential crisis; so he reminded Zhou Wang to pay attention to Ji Chang. However, Zhou Wang firmly believed that Ji Chang only had mediocre ability, and Jiang Ziya was deliberately full of hot air. Both of them were not worth mentioning.

Zhou Wang had built several magnificent examples of architecture to amuse Daji, including the Star Picking

Pavilion, the Pond of Wine with Forest of Meat, and the Deer Stage. Daji cheated Zhou Wang that immortals would visit the Deer Stage because the place was divine. Zhou Wang had sincerely expected the immortals' visit; hence, Daji invited her fellow vixen. They were disguised as fairies and attended the banquet at the Deer Stage.

比干除妖

姬昌回到西岐後，他的威望日漸增長。姜子牙的協助也使得西岐成為了極為繁盛的諸侯國。紂王的叔叔比干意識到潛在的危機，所以他向紂王進言要小心姬昌。但是紂王卻深信姬昌能力平庸，姜子牙裝神弄鬼，兩個人都不值得一提。

紂王先後建造了幾棟宏偉的建築為妲己享樂，包括摘星樓、酒池肉林和鹿台。妲己唬弄紂王說，因為鹿台非常神聖，會有神仙降臨。紂王對神仙降臨期待不已，所以妲己邀請了她的同伴狐狸精，她們扮成神仙的樣子來鹿台赴宴。

文法正誤句

KEY 33

Jiang Ziya's help also made Xiqi <u>a more prosperous kingdom</u>.

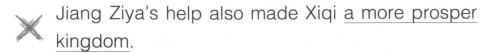
Jiang Ziya's help also made Xiqi <u>a more prosper kingdom.</u>

中譯 姜子牙的協助也使得西岐成為了極為繁盛的諸侯國。

解析 Prosperous 是形容詞繁榮的、興旺的；而 prosper 是不及物動詞，表示富有、繁盛的意思。

KEY 34

Zhou Wang's uncle Bigan realized the potential crisis; so he reminded Zhou Wang <u>to pay attention to</u> Ji Chang.

Zhou Wang's uncle Bigan realized the potential crisis; so he reminded Zhou Wang <u>to draw attention to</u> Ji Chang.

中譯 紂王的叔叔比干察覺到潛在的危機，所以他向紂王進言要小心姬昌。

解析 Pay attention to 是留心、注意某事；draw attention 也有吸引……注意的意思。但 pay attention to sb/sth 是單純的將注意力放在某人／某物上，draw attention 則常用於 draw attention away from sth，把注意力從……移開，分散注意力，也可以說 draw sb's attention，引起某人注意。

KEY 35

Zhou Wang had built several magnificent examples of architecture to amuse Daji, including the Star Picking Pavilion, the Pond of Wine with Forest of Meat, and the Deer Stage.

Zhou Wang had built several magnificent examples of architecture to amuse Daji, included the Star Picking Pavilion, the Pond of Wine with Forest of Meat, and the Deer Stage.

中譯 紂王先後建造了幾棟宏偉的建築為妲己享樂，包括摘星樓、酒池肉林和鹿台。

解析 Including 和 included 意義相同，有主動和被動的差別，一般 including 放在包含的東西前面做修飾，而 included 放在列舉各項內容之後。

KEY 36

Daji invited her fellow vixen, they were disguised as fairies and attended the banquet at the Deer Stage.

Daji invited her fellow vixen, they disguised as fairies and attend to the banquet at the Deer Stage.

中譯 妲己邀請了她同類狐狸精，他們扮成神仙的樣子來鹿台赴宴。

解析 Disguise 做動詞意思不是喬裝，而是使喬裝，是及物動

75

詞，因而不能沒有受詞。可以寫作 they disguised themselves as fairies 或 they were disguised as fairies。而不能說 they disguised as fairies。

9-2 封神榜小故事 | MP3 18
狐狸皮衣

Fox fur clothes

As Zhou Wang's uncle, Bigan was invited to join the banquet. Those foxes had never seen such a sumptuous feast, they guzzled all the dishes on the tables. Some foxes indulged in binge drinking and got drunk; then they displayed their original figures as foxes. Zhou Wang was unsuspecting of the abnormality of those 'immortals'; but Bigan, on the contrary, observed everything clearly and felt extremely disappointed. After the banquet, Bigan ordered a group of soldiers to follow those foxes back to the Xuanyuan Tomb. The soldiers set a fire and burnt all the drunk vixens to death. Bigan made fur clothes from the collected fox corpses. He sent the clothes to Zhou Wang and Daji as a warning. Daji vowed to avenge this wrong after seeing those fur clothes made by Bigan.

狐狸皮衣

比干作為皇叔也被邀請參加宴會。狐狸們從沒見過那麼豐盛的美食，她們吃掉所有桌上的食物。一些狐狸酒喝太多醉倒，露出了狐狸原形。紂王對這些「神仙」的異常狀況渾然不覺，比干卻看得清清楚楚並且感到極為失望。晚宴過後，比干命令一隊士兵跟蹤狐狸們回到了軒轅墳。士兵們放火燒墳，把所有喝醉的狐狸都燒死了。比干以狐狸屍體製成了皮衣。妲己看到那些比干所製的皮後對發誓要報仇。

「文法出題要點」

（　）1. Those foxes had never seen _____ sumptuous feast, they guzzled all the dishes on the tables.

（A）such a

（B）a such

（C）such as

（D）so such

答　　案	A
題目中譯	狐狸們從沒見過那麼豐盛的美食，她們大吃掉所有桌上的食物。
文法重點	Such 的用法。
關鍵知識	Such a (an)+形容詞＋單數可數名詞做定語
文法解析	Such 應該放在 a/an 之前，但放在 some, any, no,

every 之後。Such as 則是用作舉例。

( ) 2. Some foxes indulged in binge drinking and went _____; then then they displayed their original figures as foxes..

（A）drank　　　　　　（B）drink
（C）drunken　　　　　（D）drunk

答　案　D

題目中譯　一些狐狸酒喝太多醉倒，露出了狐狸原形。

文法重點　drunk 跟 drunken 的用法。

關鍵知識　形容詞 drunk 意思是喝醉的，drunken 則是常酗酒的意思。

文法解析　Went 後面需要接過去分詞，只有 drunken 和 drunk 兩個選擇，drunk 在此處符合狐狸赴宴喝醉酒的意思。

( ) 3. Zhou Wang was unaware of the _____ of those 'immortals'; but Bigan observed everything clearly and felt extremely disappointed.

（A）atypical　　　　　（B）uncommon
（C）abnormal　　　　　（D）abnormality

答　　案　　D

題目中譯　紂王對這些「神仙」的異常狀況渾然不覺，比干卻看得清清楚楚並且感到極為失望。

文法重點　Be unaware of sth，介系詞＋名詞。

關鍵知識　沒有意識到或沒有覺察到的事實應當是名詞。

文法解析　只有 abmormality 是一個名詞，其餘選項都是形容詞。

（　）4. After the banquet, Bigan ordered a group of soldiers _____ those foxes back to the Xuanyuan Tomb.

（A）follows 　　　　　　（B）follow
（C）to follow 　　　　　（D）following

答　　案　　C

題目中譯　比干命令一隊士兵跟蹤狐狸們回到了軒轅墳。

文法重點　命令某人做某事的用法。

關鍵知識　Order sb to do sth 要用不定詞。

文法解析　Order sb 後面要接不定詞，不可以加名詞原形或動名詞。

Unit 10

比干

慣用語、副詞連接詞

10-1 封神榜小故事 | MP3 19
七竅玲瓏心

A heart with seven apertures／七竅玲瓏心

One day, Daji complained she had vomited blood. Zhou Wang tried to find her a cure desperately. Daji told Zhou Wang that her illness was terminal; the only cure was a remedy that was made of 'a heart with seven apertures'.

When Bigan was young, Master Merciful Navigation (慈航道人) gave him the seven apertures heart as an amulet. People who have this heart possess supreme wisdom. In addition, the heart protects the person against evil spirits. Zhou Wang knew that Bigan was the only person with the seven apertures heart; so he ordered Bigan to dedicate his heart to Daji.

Jiang Ziya once forecasted that Zhou Wang and Daji would claim Bigan's heart, so he left Bigan a talisman, which would protect Bigan's life when he lost his heart. Jiang Ziya told Bigan to burn the talisman, eat the ashes, and keep walking towards the south until he reaches a safe place.

 ## 七竅玲瓏心

有一天，妲己抱怨說她會吐血。紂王竭盡全力想要為妲己找到治療方法。妲己就告訴紂王自己已經病入膏肓，唯一的救命藥需要「七竅玲瓏心」做藥材。

比干小時候，慈航道人賜給他七竅玲瓏心做護身符。擁有七竅玲瓏心的人有極高的智慧，神符也保護主人不受邪魔侵害。紂王知道比干是唯一擁有「七竅玲瓏心」的人，於是他命令比干將心獻給妲己。

姜子牙曾預知紂王和妲己會向比干要他的心；所以他為比干留下一副護身符，可以為比干在失去心臟時保命。姜子牙告訴比干要燒掉靈符，把灰燼吃下去，一直向南走，直到到達安全的地方就可以得救。

文法正誤句

○ Zhou Wang tried to find her a cure <u>desperately</u>.

✗ Zhou Wang tried to find her a cure <u>desperate</u>.

中譯 紂王竭盡全力想要為妲己找到治療方法。

解析 急切地想要做一件事，可以說 be desperate to do sth 或 do sth desperately。Desperate 是形容詞，修飾動詞需要用副詞。

○ Daji told Zhou Wang that her illness was terminal; the only cure was a remedy that <u>was made of</u> 'a heart with seven apertures'.

✗ Daji told Zhou Wang that her illness was terminal; the only cure was a remedy that <u>was made from</u> 'a heart with seven apertures'.

中譯 妲己就告訴紂王自己已經病入膏肓，唯一的救命藥需要「七竅玲瓏心」做藥材。

解析 Be made of 和 be made from 的微妙區別是：倘若製造過程中發生了化學反應或本質的改變，就常用 made from，例如：Bread is made from flour；如果單純是一

種材料製成成品，中間沒有化學轉變，就常用 made of，例如：The table is made of wood。此處的狀況應當是用 be made of。

KEY 39

○ Zhou Wang knew that Bigan was the only person with the seven apertures heart, so he ordered Bigan to dedicate his heart to Daji.

✗ Zhou Wang knew that Bigan was the only person with the seven apertures heart, so he ordered Bigan to dedicate to Daji.

中譯 紂王知道比干是唯一擁有「七竅玲瓏心」的人，於是他命令比干將心獻給妲己。

解析 Dedicate 奉獻是一個及物動詞，後面需附加被獻上的內容，如時間、心血、精力等。這個句子中 dedicate 要加上受詞 his heart。

KEY 40

○ So he left Bigan a talisman, which would protect Bigan's life when he lost his heart.

✗ So he left Bigan a talisman, that would protect Bigan's life when he lost his heart.

中譯 所以他為比干留下一副護身符，可以為比干失去心臟時保命。

這個句子是一個非限定性形容詞子句,即關係代詞引導的子句即使省略,也不影響主句的意思,只是單純對主句做進一步解釋說明。在非限定性形容詞子句中,關係代詞一般只會用 which 和 who,不可以用 that。

10-2 封神榜小故事 | 🎵 MP3 20

無心菜

 vegetable without heart

Bigan entered the palace after eating the talisman's ashes. Condemning Zhou Wang for being a fatuous tyrant, he then dug out his heart and handed it to Zhou Wang. After that, Bigan held his hand over the hole in his chest, left the palace, and walked towards the south. He tried to ignore everyone he saw merely concentrating on walking. Nevertheless, an old woman selling vegetables had caught his attention. The woman was selling water spinach - a vegetable without a heart. Not knowing what that vegetable she was selling, Bigan asked the woman, 'What is the name of the vegetable?' The woman told Bigan that it was hallow vegetable, she said, vegetable without heart is edible, but man without heart is lethal. These words broke the power of the talisman, making

Bigan suddenly realize that he was a man without a heart, and he died at the scene.

無心菜

　　比干吃下靈符的灰後進入了皇宮。他譴責紂王是昏庸的暴君，並挖出自己的心交給了紂王。這之後，比干用手摀著胸口的洞，離開了皇宮向南走去。他試著忽略所有遇見的人，只專注於走路。儘管如此，一個賣菜的老婦人還是吸引了他的注意。這位老婦賣的是空心菜。因為不知道老婦賣什麼菜，比干問她：「這菜叫什麼名字？」老婦告訴比干那是空心菜，她說：「菜無心可以吃，人無心則要死。」這句話打破了護身符的法力，比干突然意識到自己是個沒有心的人，當場死去了。

「文法出題要點」

（　　）1. Bigan entered the palace ＿＿＿＿＿ he ate the talisman's ashes.

　　　　（A）before　　　　　　（B）after
　　　　（C）since　　　　　　　（D）when

答　　案　　B

題目中譯　　比干吃下靈符的灰後進入了皇宮。

文法重點　　表示時間的介詞。

關鍵知識　從邏輯上判斷比干應當是吃下靈符後再進入皇宮，所以時間順序上應當用 after。

文法解析　After 是在……之後，before 是在……之前，since 表示自從……，when 是當……時候，只有 after 符合此處的句意。

(　　) 2. After that, Bigan held his hand over the hole in his chest, left the palace and _____ towards the south.

　　　　(A) walked　　　　　　(B) walks

　　　　(C) walk　　　　　　　(D) had walked

答　　案　A

題目中譯　這之後，比干用手捂著胸口的洞，離開了皇宮向南走去。

文法重點　動詞的一貫性。

關鍵知識　一個句子中幾個並列的動詞應當用同樣的時態。

文法解析　Held, left 和 walked 是三個連續的、並列發生的動作，故 walked 與其他兩個字的時態一致，故用過去式。

(　　) 3. _____, an old woman selling vegetables had caught his attention.

（A）Although
（B）In spite of
（C）Rather
（D）Nevetheless

答　案　D

題目中譯　儘管如此，一個賣菜的老婦人還是吸引了他的注意。

文法重點　轉折副詞的用法

關鍵知識　However 表示然而，有強烈的轉折意味。

文法解析　Although 和 rather 都不可以用逗號隔開單獨使用，in spite of 後面應當接一個詞而非句子。只有 however 從文法和意義上都符合此處的要求。

（　）4. Vegetable without heart is edible, but man without heart is ＿＿＿＿＿＿.

（A）vigorous
（B）robust
（C）lethal
（D）healthy

答　案　C

題目中譯　菜無心可以吃，人無心則要死。

文法重點　依據上下文判斷用字。

關鍵知識　由比干聽到老太婆的話就氣絕身亡，判斷出老太婆的意思應該是沒有心就不能活。

文法解析　除了 lethal，其餘選項都是健康強壯的意思。

Unit *11*

黃飛虎

關係代名詞、同位語

11-1 封神榜小故事 | MP3 21

黃飛虎投奔西岐

Huang Feihu sought asylum in Xiqi

General Huang Feihu was born into a family which served the Shang Dynasty loyally for generations. Huang Feihu's younger sister was Zhou Wang's concubines. One day, Huang Feihu's wife Lady Jia visited Consort Huang in the palace; but Zhou Wang harassed Lady Jia and attempted to seize her as his concubine as well. Lady Jia felt humiliated and killed herself to preserve her dignity. Seeing the suicide of her sister-in-law, Consort Huang scolded Zhou Wang for his unscrupulous behavior. Zhou Wang went mad and pulled Consort

Huang off a building.

Huang Feihu was extremely angry after learning of the death of his wife and sister. He ran into the palace and fought with Zhou Wang. <u>Huang Feihu's moral principles prevented him from killing the king</u>, so after beating Zhou Wang down, he defected to Xiqi. <u>All of Huang Feihu's faithful followers accompanied him to Xiqi.</u>

 ## 黃飛虎投奔西岐

　　黃飛虎將軍出生於一個世代效忠商王朝的家庭。黃飛虎的妹妹是紂王的皇妃。一天，黃飛虎的妻子賈夫人去宮中和黃妃見面，但是紂王騷擾賈夫人還想要把她留下做自己的妃了。賈夫人感到被侮辱，就自殺以求尊嚴。看到大嫂自殺，黃妃責罵紂王行為不道德，紂王發怒把黃妃從樓下推了下去。

　　得知夫人和妹妹的死訊，黃飛虎極為憤怒。他衝入皇宮和紂王大戰。黃飛虎的道德準則令他不能弒君，所以他打倒紂王後，就去投奔西岐。黃飛虎忠誠的下屬們也都跟著他一起去了西岐。

文法正誤句

KEY 41

○ General Huang Feihu was born into <u>a family which</u> served the Shang Dynasty loyally for generations.

✕ General Huang Feihu was born into <u>a family who</u> served the Shang Dynasty loyally for generations.

中譯 黃飛虎將軍出生於一個世代效忠商王朝的家庭。

解析 形容詞子句的關係代詞 which 修飾先行詞 family，子句的主詞指代黃飛虎的家庭，因而要用 which 而不可以用 who。

KEY 42

○ Consort Huang <u>scolded</u> Zhou Wang <u>for his</u> <u>unscrupulous behavior</u>.

✕ Consort Huang <u>praised</u> Zhou Wang <u>for his</u> <u>unscrupulous behavior</u>.

中譯 黃妃責罵紂王行為不道德。

解析 不道德的行為受到的是責罵而非讚賞，所以應當是 scold 嚴詞責罵，不是 praise。

KEY 43

○ Huang Feihu's moral principles prevented him from killing the king.

✗ Huang Feihu's moral principles prevented him to kill the king.

中譯 黃飛虎的道德準則令他不能弒君。

解析 阻止某人做某事的慣用法是 prevent sb from doing sth，其中 from 可以省略。不能用 prevent sb to do sth。

KEY 44

○ All of Huang Feihu's faithful followers accompanied him to Xiqi.

✗ All of Huang Feihu's faithful followers accompanied him to flee to Xiqi.

中譯 黃飛虎忠誠的下屬們也都跟著他一起去了西岐。

解析 陪伴某人做某事不能說 accompany sb to do sth。要表示陪同某人去某地，只需要說 accompany sb to somewhere。

Huang Feihu was captured

On their way towards the west, Huang Feihu and his people encountered several barriers guarded by mighty opponents. Chen Tong (陳桐) in the Tong Pass (潼關) hit Huang Feihu with concealed venom weapons and poisoned him. Daode Zhenjun (道德真君) sent his apprentice Huang Tianhua (黃天化), Huang Feihu's son, to collect Chen Tong's hidden weapons with a flower basket and assist Huang Feihu to pass the block. The biggest crisis on their way occurred in Sishui Pass (氾水關). Yu Hua, (余化) the border protector, was an expert in witchcraft. He captured Huang's whole family and planned to send them back to Zhou Wang. Nezha defeated Yu Hua and escorted the Huang Family to arrive in Xiqi. Wu Wang delightfully welcomed them and conferred Huang Feihu the title of Wucheng King (武成王).

 黃飛虎遭擒

在西行路上，黃飛虎一行人遇到幾個有強大對手防衛的關卡。潼關的陳桐用有毒暗器打中黃飛虎，令他中毒。道德真君派弟子黃天，

黃飛虎的兒子用花籃收了陳桐的暗器，並協助黃飛虎過關。黃飛虎路上最大的危機出現在氾水關。氾水關守將余化是一位擅長妖術的專家。余化俘虜了黃飛虎全家，要把他們押解回去獻給紂王。哪吒打敗了余化，並護送黃飛虎到達了西岐。武王高興地迎接了他們，並冊封黃飛虎為武成王。

 「文法出題要點」

（　）1. Huang Feihu and his people encountered several barriers ＿＿＿＿＿ by mighty opponents.

    （A）that guarded   （B）guarded

    （C）were guarded   （D）that were guard

答　　案　B

題目中譯　黃飛虎一行人遇到幾個有強大對手防衛的關卡。

文法重點　分詞起形容詞的作用，修飾名詞。

關鍵知識　Guarded by mighty opponents 可以直接修飾 barriers，表示這些關卡有強大的對手防衛。

文法解析　另一種說法可以是 barriers that were guarded by mighty opponents，用形容詞子句修飾 barriers，此時 guarded 是動詞的被動態。而 that guarded 和 were guarded 是錯誤的用法。

（　）2. Chen Tong in the Tong Pass hit Huang Feihu with concealed venom weapons and ＿＿＿＿＿ him.

（A）poisoned   （B）poison

（C）toxic   （D）intoxicated

答　案	A
題目中譯	潼關的陳桐用有毒暗器打中黃飛虎，令他中毒。
文法重點	中毒的説法。
關鍵知識	Poison 有名詞毒物和動詞下毒、使中毒的意思。
文法解析	事件於過去發生的，poison 要用過去式。Intoxicated 原意是被酒精或藥物麻痺了神經，引申為陶醉、專注於某件事。

（　）3. Daode Zhenjun sent his apprentice Huang Tianhua , Huang Feihu's son, to collect Chen Tong's hidden weapons with a flower basket and ＿＿＿＿＿ Huang Feihu to pass the block.

（A）has assisted   （B）had assisted

（C）assisted   （D）assist

答　案	D
題目中譯	道德真君派弟子黃天化用花籃收了陳桐的暗器，並協助

黃飛虎過關。

文法重點　and 隔開兩個被不定時修飾的動詞。

關鍵知識　不定詞是 to 後加原形動詞。

文法解析　收暗器和協助這兩個動作都是 to do 的內容，雖然中間
　　　　　被 and 隔開，但 collect 和 assist 都要用原形動詞。

（　）4. Yu Hua, _____ , was an expert in witchcraft.

（A）which

（B）whom

（C）who thc border protector

（D）the border protector

答　案　D

題目中譯　汜水關守將余化是一位擅長妖術的專家。

文法重點　同位語的用法。

關鍵知識　同位語的本身是名詞或名詞片語，放在另一個名詞旁
　　　　　邊，當作幫助說明的作用。

文法解析　同位語放在先行詞後面，它可以取代先行詞。只有 D
　　　　　選項 the border protector 可以完全取代 Yu Hua
　　　　　這個詞，是 Yu Hua 的非限定性同位語。

Unit 12

哪吒

名詞、指示代名詞、副詞連接詞

12-1 封神榜小故事 | MP3 23
哪吒大戰張桂芳

Nezha fought with Zhang Guifang (張桂芳)

Seeing Huang Feihu's defection, many generals also decided to serve Wu Wang instead of Zhou Wang. The Grand Master (太師) Wen Zhong (聞仲) suggested Zhou Wang send forces to suppress Xiqi. Zhou Wang then ordered Zhang Guifang, the commander of Green Dragon Pass (青龍關), to Xiqi on a punitive campaign.

Huang Feihu reminded Jiang Ziya that Zhang Guifang wielded a magical ability. With this ability, Zhang Guifang could manipulate that person by calling out one's name. Zhang Guifang was confronted by Jiang Ziya who persuaded him into serving the Shang Empire. After he refused him, Jiang Ziya sent several generals to fight with Zhang Guifang. <u>Whenever Zhang Guifang called out names, Xiqi's generals would fall from their horses and be captured.</u>

 ## 哪吒大戰張桂芳

看到黃飛虎反叛後，許多將軍也選擇了為武王效力，離開紂王。太師聞仲建議紂王派兵去討伐西岐。於是紂王命令青龍關守將張桂芳前去西岐討伐武王。

黃飛虎提醒姜子牙，張桂芳會使用超能力。有了這種能力，張桂芳呼喚一個人的名字就可以控制他的意識。張桂芳見到姜子牙後就勸他為商王朝效命，姜子牙拒絕後派出幾員大將對戰張桂芳。每次張桂芳叫出名字後，西岐的將軍都會從馬上跌下來被俘虜。

 ## 文法正誤句

 ## KEY 45

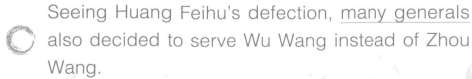

Seeing Huang Feihu's defection, <u>many generals</u> also decided to serve Wu Wang instead of Zhou Wang.

Seeing Huang Feihu's defection, <u>much generals</u> also decided to serve Wu Wang instead of Zhou Wang.

中譯 看到黃飛虎反叛後，許多將軍也選擇了為武王效力，離開紂王。

解析 Generals 將軍是可數名詞，用 many 來修飾；much 後面應當接不可數名詞。

🔥 KEY 46

Zhou Wang then ordered Zhang Guifang, <u>the commander of Green Dragon Pass,</u> to Xiqi on a punitive campaign.

Zhou Wang then ordered Zhang Guifang <u>the commander of Green Dragon Pass</u> to Xiqi on a punitive campaign.

中譯 於是紂王命令青龍關守將張桂芳前去西岐討伐武王。

解析 非限定性同位語前後都應該有逗號分隔開。

🔥 KEY 47

With this ability, Zhang Guifang could <u>manipulate that person by calling out one's name.</u>

With this ability, Zhang Guifang could <u>manipulate this person by calling out one's name.</u>

中譯 有了這種能力，張桂芳呼喚一個人的名字就可以控制他的意識。

解析 That 和 those 可以代替前面說過的名詞，而 this 和 these 沒有這種用法。

KEY 48

○ Every times after Zhang Guifang called out names, Xiqi's generals <u>would fall from their horses and be captured.</u>

✗ Every times after Zhang Guifang called out names, Xiqi's generals <u>would fall from their horses and captured.</u>

中譯 每次張桂芳叫出名字後，西岐的將軍都會從馬上跌下來被俘虜。

解析 被俘獲應當用被動語態 be captured。

12-2 封神榜小故事｜ MP3 24
哪吒打敗張桂芳

Nezha defeated Zhang Guifang

<u>Jiang Ziya had no choice but to deal with this situation.</u> He fled to Kunlun Mountain and asked his

teacher the Primeval Lord of Heaven (元始天尊) for a clue. The Lord reassured Jiang Ziya that a kindhearted king would never be defeated by sorcery. Aids would always present themselves at critical moments.

When Jiang Ziya returned to the battle field, he found Nezha had joined the Xiqi army. Nezha requested a duel with Zhang Guifang. They had a big fight for several rounds and Zhang Guifang shouted loudly, Nezha, get down from your wheels! However, Not only did Nezha not fall from his Wind Fire Wheels, but he gave Zhang Guifang's a crucial attack by using his Universe Ring. Everyone was surprised that Zhang Guifang's witchcraft had lost its mind-control power. Nezha told Jiang Ziya that he was made from a lotus; hence, Zhang Guifang's sorcery would not do the trick.

 ## 哪吒打敗張桂芳

姜子牙不得不面對問題，他遁去崑崙山向師父元始天尊請教對付張桂芳方法。天尊安慰姜子牙説，仁義之君是不會被妖術打敗的，危難之時必然有人出手相救。

姜子牙回到戰場，就發現哪吒加入了西岐軍。哪吒要求和張桂芳對戰，兩人大戰了幾個回合後，張桂芳大叫道：「哪吒快從輪子上掉

下來！」沒想到哪吒不僅沒有從風火輪摔下來，反倒用乾坤圈重傷了張桂芳。眾人都十分驚訝張桂芳巫術失去了精神控制的效用。哪吒告訴姜子牙由於他是蓮花化身，所以張桂芳的妖術無法控制他。

 「文法出題要點」

（　）1. Jiang Ziya had no choice but ＿＿＿＿＿with this situation.

　　（A）deals 　　　　　　（B）to deal
　　（C）dealing 　　　　　（D）deal

答　　案	B
題目中譯	姜子牙不得不面對問題。
文法重點	不得不的用法。
關鍵知識	表示不得不可以用 can't help but＋原形動詞，can't help doing 或 have no choice but to＋原形動詞。
文法解析	B 選項符合 have no choice but to do sth 的固定用法。

（　）2. The Lord reassured Jiang Ziya that a kindhearted king would never ＿＿＿＿＿＿ sorcery.

（A）defeating （B）defeats by

（C）defeat （D）be defeated by

答　　案	D
題目中譯	天尊安慰姜子牙說，仁義之君是不會被妖術打敗的。
文法重點	Defeat，擊敗的過去分詞。
關鍵知識	被……打敗為 be defeated by sth。
文法解析	C 選項在文法上正確，但意義上是錯誤的，只有 D 選項是正確的選擇。

（　）3. When Jiang Ziya returned to the battle field, he found Nezha _____ the Xiqi army.

（A）has joined （B）joins

（C）joined （D）had joined

答　　案	D
題目中譯	姜子牙回到戰場，就發現哪吒加入了西岐軍。
文法重點	過去完成式。
關鍵知識	過去完成式為 had＋過去分詞。
文法解析	完成式表示一件事發生在另一件事之前，在姜子牙回到戰場之前，哪吒已經加入了西岐軍隊，所以用完成式。而整個句子都是過去式，所以此處應是過去完成式。

（ 　 ） 4. Nezha told Jiang Ziya that he was made from a lotus; _____, Zhang Guifang's sorcery would not do the trick.

（A）in addition 　　　（B）nevertheless

（C）however 　　　　（D）hence

答　　案　　D

題目中譯　　哪吒告訴姜子牙由於他是蓮花化身，所以張桂芳的妖術無法控制他。

文法重點　　連接副詞的用法。

關鍵知識　　連接副詞的用法接近對等連接詞，可以連接兩個獨立的句子。

文法解析　　In addition 表示遞進，nevertheless 和 however 表示轉折，只有 hence 表示因果關係。

Unit 13

姜子牙
慣用語、動詞、條件句

13-1 封神榜小故事 | 🎧 MP3 25
姜子牙險失封神榜

Jiang Ziya almost lost the 'Investiture of Gods Volume' ／姜子牙險失封神榜

When Jiang Ziya was on the Kunlun Mountain consulting the strategies of fighting Zhang Guifang, the Primeval Lord of Heaven gave him the 'Investiture of Gods Volume'. The Lord told Jiang Ziya to protect the volume carefully and build the 'Investiture of Gods Platform' in the Qi Mountain near Xiqi.

On his way back to Xiqi, Jiang Ziya heard someone call his name from behind. Jiang Ziya was quite vigilant about name-calling after fighting with Zhang Guifang. He turned with great caution and found out the voice was from his junior apprentice Shen Gongbao (申公豹). Shen Gongbao served Zhou Wang and regarded Jiang Ziya as an enemy. When Shen Gongbao saw the Investiture of Gods Volume in Jiang Ziya's hand, he decided to seize it.

姜子牙險失封神榜

姜子牙上崑崙山求助對付張桂芳的策略時，元始天尊交給他一部「封神榜」。元始天尊囑咐姜子牙小心保管「封神榜」，並且要在西岐旁邊的岐山建造「封神台」。

姜子牙在趕回西岐途中，聽到有人在背後叫自己的名字。由於吃過張桂芳的苦頭，姜子牙對喊名字非常警覺。他小心翼翼地轉身後，才發現原來聲音來自他的師弟申公豹。申公豹為紂王效力，把姜子牙當作對手。當申公豹看到姜子牙手中的封神榜，就想把它據為己有。

文法正誤句

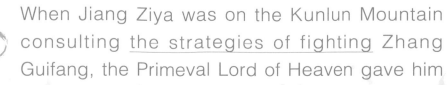

KEY 49

When Jiang Ziya was on the Kunlun Mountain consulting the strategies of fighting Zhang Guifang, the Primeval Lord of Heaven gave him the Investiture of Gods Volume.

When Jiang Ziya was on the Kunlun Mountain consulting the strategies of fight Zhang Guifang, the Primeval Lord of Heaven gave him the 'Investiture of Gods Volume'.

中譯 姜子牙上崑崙山求助對付張桂芳的策略時，元始天尊交給他一部「封神榜」。

解析 動詞接在介系詞之後應當加 ing 變成動名詞。

KEY 50

The Lord told Jiang Ziya to protect the volume carefully and build the Investiture of Gods Platform in the Qi Mountain near Xiqi.

The Lord told Jiang Ziya to protect the volume carefully and builded the Investiture of Gods Platform in the Qi Mountain near Xiqi.

中譯 元始天尊囑咐姜子牙小心保管「封神榜」並且要在西岐旁邊的岐山建造「封神台」。

解析 Protect 和 build 都是 tell Jiang Ziya to do 的內容，兩個動詞都要用原形動詞。

KEY 51

He turned <u>with caution</u> and found out the voice was from his junior apprentice Shen Gongbao.

He turned <u>with cautious</u> and found out the voice was from his junior apprentice Shen Gongbao.

中譯 他小心轉身看才發現原來聲音來自他的師弟申公豹。

解析 小心轉身的 with 後應當接一個名詞，而 cautious 是形容詞。

KEY 52

Shen Gongbao served Zhou Wang and regarded Jiang Ziya as <u>an enemy.</u>

Shen Gongbao served Zhou Wang and regarded Jiang Ziya as <u>a enemy</u>.

中譯 申公豹為紂王效力，把姜子牙當作對手。

解析 不定冠詞 a 後面的名詞以輔音字母開頭，而 an 後面的名詞以母音字母開頭。

打賭

The bet

Shen Gongbao made a bet with Jiang Ziya, 'Now I am going to chop off my head. Then if I am still alive, you should burn down the volume in your hand and follow me to serve Zhou Wang.' Jiang Ziya wondered whether Shen Gongbao could manage to survive without a head, so he agreed to the deal.

When Shen Gongbao threw his head into the sky, the immortal of the South Pole (南極仙翁), who coincidently was passing by just then found Shen Gongbao's head flying in the air weirdly. Realizing that this was a trick, the Immortal of the South Pole asked his apprentice the White Crane Boy (白鶴童子) to carry away Shen Gongbao's head; he also warned Jiang Ziya to burn down Shen Gongbao's body in no time. Jiang Ziya then realized that he was fooled. But Jiang Ziya was reluctant to kill his fellow apprentice Shen Gongbao; he requested the White Crane Boy to return the head to Shen Gongbao.

打賭

申公豹跟姜子牙打賭說：「現在我要將自己的頭砍下來，如果我還活著，你就要燒掉手裡的封神榜，和我一起去輔佐紂王。」姜子牙想知道申公豹是否能做得到沒有頭還能生存，就答應了他。

申公豹砍下自己的頭拋到了空中。剛好此時南極仙翁路過，他看到申公豹的頭在天上飛得很怪，就覺察出一定有詐。南極仙翁要徒弟白鶴童子叼走申公豹的頭，他也告誡姜子牙立即燒掉申公豹的身體。姜子牙這才發現自己被騙了。但姜子牙不忍心燒死同門師弟申公豹，他請求白鶴童子把申公豹的頭還回他的身體。

「文法出題要點」

（　）1. Shen Gongbao made a _____ with Jiang
　　　 Ziya.

　　（A）price 　　　　　（B）guess
　　（C）bet 　　　　　（D）wish

答　案	C
題目中譯	申公豹對姜子牙打賭。
文法重點	Make a ...
關鍵知識	由 make a＋名詞組成的片語有很多，如 make a

bargain 成交，make a bet 打賭，make a call 訪問，make a choice 選擇，make a face 做鬼臉，make a feast 請客等。

A make a price 表示定價，B make a guess 是做猜測，D make a wish 是許願。C 是正確選項。

( ) 2. Then if _____ still alive, you should burn down the volume in your hand and follow me to serve Zhou Wang.

(A) I am   (B) I would be

(C) I will be   (D) I was

答　案　A

題目中譯　如果我還活著，你就要燒掉手裡的封神榜，和我一起去輔佐紂王。

文法重點　If 條件句。

關鍵知識　If 條件句表示對未來事情的假設時，主句用將來時，if 子句用一般現在式。

文法解析　A 是一般現在式，其他選項則是將來式和過去式。

( ) 3. He also warned Jiang Ziya to burn down Shen Gongbao's body _____.

（A）at times   （B）on time

（C）in time   （D）in no time

答　　案	D
題目中譯	他也告誡姜子牙立即燒掉申公豹的身體。
文法重點	帶 time 的片語。
關鍵知識	in no time 表示立刻、馬上。
文法解析	At times 是偶爾，on time 表示準時，in time 表示及時。

（　）4. Jiang Ziya then realized that he was ＿＿＿＿＿ .

（A）a fool   （B）foolish

（C）fool   （D）fooled

答　　案	D
題目中譯	姜子牙這才發現自己被騙了。
文法重點	fool 的相關用法。
關鍵知識	Fool 用作動詞是欺騙、愚弄的意思；做名詞表示傻瓜；做形容詞表示傻的。
文法解析	此處是 fool 用作動詞，表示被欺騙，上當的意思。

Unit 14

姜子牙

關係代名詞、被動語態

14-1 封神榜小故事 | MP3 27
姜子牙收徒龍鬚虎

Jiang Ziya took Dragon Beard Tiger as apprentice

The Grand Master Wen Zhong was informed of Zhang Guifang's failure; then he rode his Black Chinese Unicorn to the Nine Dragons Island where four masters lived. The four masters all had scary appearances. When they arrived with their respective mythical beasts, all the Xiqi soldiers and horses were daunted. Jiang Ziya immediately sought help from his master the Primeval Lord of Heaven for help. This time he granted a Milu Deer - Sibuxiang (四不像) to ride, a magical whip which was able to beat any immortal, and a apricot coloured flag for self-protection.

With those weapons in hand, Jiang Ziya returned to Xiqi. When he passed the Northern Sea, a monster jumped out and tried to eat him. The monster was named Dragon Beard Tiger. It had sharp claws and sparkling flakes over its body. Jiang Ziya calmed himself down and thrusted the apricot coloured flag into the ground. He told the monster, you can eat me if you are able to pull the flag out! Dragon Beard Tiger made his best endeavor, but failed to remove the flag. The monster was also shocked that the flag was glued on its claw.

 ## 姜子牙收徒龍鬚虎

聞太師得知張桂芳戰敗，他騎著墨麒麟前往有四位高人的九龍島。四位大師都長相嚇人。當他們騎著各自的神獸到來時，西岐所有的將士和馬匹都被嚇壞了。姜子牙急忙找他的師父元始天尊求助，這一次他得到了坐騎「四不像」，武器「打神鞭」，和護身的杏黃旗。

得到這些武器後，姜子牙返回西岐。他路過北海時，一隻妖怪跳出來要吃他。這隻叫做龍鬚虎的妖怪長著尖爪，渾身佈滿閃亮的鱗片。姜子牙鎮定下來，將杏黃旗用力插到地上。他對妖怪說：「如果你可以把這面旗拔出來，就可以吃我！」龍鬚虎竭盡全力去拔旗，但是無法成功。妖怪也因為自己的爪子和旗子黏在一起大吃一驚。

KEY 53

Then he rode his Black Unicorn to the Nine Dragons Island where four masters lived.

Then he rode his Black Unicorn to the Nine Dragons Island when four masters lived.

中譯 他騎著墨麒麟前往有四位高人的九龍島。

解析 由於先行詞「九龍島」是一個地名，而非時間。所以關係副詞為 where。

KEY 54

When they arrived with their mythical beasts; all the Xiqi soldiers and horses were daunted.

When they arrived with their mythical beasts; all the Xiqi soldiers and horses daunted.

中譯 當他們騎著各自的神獸到來時，西岐所有的將士和馬匹都被嚇壞了。

解析 Daunt 為及物動詞，表示使畏懼，一般用於被動語態：to be daunted by sth。

KEY 55

It had sharp claws and sparkling flakes <u>over its</u> <u>body</u>.

It had sharp claws and sparkling flakes <u>over it's</u> <u>body</u>.

中譯 它長著尖爪，渾身佈滿閃亮的鱗片。

解析 It's 是 it is 或 it has 的縮寫，是主詞＋系詞結構；而 its 是 it 的所有格（形容詞性物主代詞），表示「它的」。

KEY 56

Dragon Beard Tiger <u>made his best endeavor</u> but failed to remove the flag.

Dragon Beard Tiger <u>made his best endeavoring</u> but failed to remove the flag.

中譯 龍鬚虎竭盡全力去拔旗，但是無法成功。

解析 Endeavor 做名詞和動詞時都表示努力、竭盡全力地意思，所以不需要特地變形為動名詞。

Jiang Ziya defeated Nine Dragons Islands masters

Dragon Beard Tiger realized that Jiang Ziya was too formidable to defeat. He apologized to Jiang Ziya and acknowledged there was a rumor that eating Jiang Ziya could lead to immortality. The rumor spreader was Shen Gongbao. Jiang Ziya accepted Dragon Beard Tiger as his apprentice bringing him back to fight with the four masters.

Dragon Beard Tiger served in the Xiqi army as vanguard and shocked the four masters with his appalling appearance. With Dragon Beard Tiger's assistance, Jiang Ziya defeated those Nine Dragons Islands masters.

 ## 姜子牙戰勝了九龍島大師們

龍鬚虎意識到姜子牙實在是難以打敗。他向姜子牙道歉，並承認有一個謠言說吃了姜子牙可以長生不死。謠言的傳播者就是申公豹。姜子牙將龍鬚虎收為徒弟，帶他回去對付四位大師。

龍鬚虎做為西岐先鋒出陣，用他的駭人外表震驚了四位大師。在龍鬚虎的幫助下，姜子牙戰勝了九龍島大師們。

 「文法出題要點」

（　）1. Dragon Beard Tiger realized that Jiang Ziya was ＿＿＿＿＿ to defeat.

（A）so formidable
（B）much formidable
（C）not formidable
（D）too formidable

答　案	D
題目中譯	龍鬚虎意識到姜子牙實在是難以打敗。
文法重點	Too … to。
關鍵知識	Too＋形容詞／副詞＋動詞不定詞結構簡稱為 too…to 結構，表示太……而無法……；太……以致於不能。
文法解析	Jiang Ziya is too formidable to defeat 就是姜子牙太強大，難以打敗他。

（　）2. He apologized to Jiang Ziya and acknowledged there was a rumor ＿＿＿＿＿ eating Jiang Ziya leads to immortality.

(A) that   (B) when

(C) what   (D) where

答　案　　A

題目中譯　他向姜子牙道歉，並承認了有一個謠言說吃了姜子牙可以長生不死。

文法重點　關係代名詞 that

關鍵知識　關係代名詞 that 兼有代名詞和連接詞的兩種作用。

文法解析　關係代名詞虎要有 who, whom, whose, which, that。這個句子裡 that 既替代先行詞 a rumour，也引導後面的關係子句。先行詞 rumour 是一種事物，所以關係代名詞只能用 that 或 which。

(   ) 3. The rumor _____ was Shen Gongbao.

(A) spreads   (B) spreading

(C) spread   (D) spreader

答　案　　D

題目中譯　謠言的傳播者就是申公豹。

文法重點　根據句子意義選擇詞性

關鍵知識　此處需要填上的詞是名詞，造謠的人。

文法解析　Spread 是一個動詞，加 er 變成做這個動作的人，應當選 D。

（　）4. Dragon Beard Tiger served Xiqi army as vanguard and _____ the four masters with his appalling appearance.

（A）was shocked　　　（B）shocks

（C）shock　　　　　　（D）shocked

答　　案　　D

題目中譯　龍鬚虎做為西岐先鋒出陣，用他的駭人外表震驚了四位大師。

文法重點　Shock 用作動詞

關鍵知識　Shock 做動詞時可以表示主動意義的使震驚、使休克；也可以表示被動含義的感到震驚、受到震動。

文法解析　此處的 shock 是表示主動的含義，龍鬚虎用駭人的外表嚇壞其他人，直接用 shock 的過去式。

聞太師

時態、情緒動詞

15-1 封神榜小故事 | 🎧 *MP3 29*

破解十絕陣

Cracking down the Ten Formations

Several punitive expeditions against Xiqi had failed. The Grand Master Wen Zhong finally decided to lead troops by himself, aiming to give Wu Wang a deadly strike. However, on the departure ceremony, Wen Zhong's fall from his Black Chinese Unicorn made everyone deem that it was an ominous sign.

Wen Zhong invited ten prominent ritual masters from the White Deer Island. The ten masters promised to subdue Jiang Ziya with their great talent. <u>They had set ten delicately designed formations with dangerous stratagems inside, planning to claim as many lives as possible.</u>

 ## 破解十絕陣

　　幾次征討西岐的軍事行動都失敗了。太師聞仲終於決定親征，目標是給武王致命的一擊。但是在出征儀式上，聞太師從墨麒麟上摔了下來，大家都覺得這是不祥之兆。

　　聞太師在白鹿島請了十位道行高深的大師，這十個人承諾會用他們的絕技制服姜子牙。他們佈下精心設計的十陣，十陣裡佈滿了危險機關，計畫盡可能的除掉許多人。

 ## 文法正誤句

 ### *KEY 57*

○ Several punitive expeditions against Xiqi <u>had failed.</u>

✗ Several punitive expeditions against Xiqi <u>had been failed</u>.

中譯 幾次征討西岐的軍事行動都失敗了。

解析　Failed 本身有形容詞的意思，表示失敗的；不必在加 be 動詞變被動語態。

KEY 58

The Grand Master Wen Zhong finally decided to lead a troop by himself, <u>aiming to give</u> Wu Wang a deadly strike.

The Grand Master Wen Zhong finally decided to lead a troop by himself, <u>aiming at give</u> Wu Wang a deadly strike.

中譯　太師聞仲終於決定親征，目標是給武王致命一擊。

解析　Aim to 和 aim at 均指立志做某事，慣用搭配是 aim to do sth 和 aim at doing sth。Aim at 也有瞄準的意思。

KEY 59

The ten masters <u>promised to subdue Jiang Ziya</u> with their great talent.

The ten masters <u>promised to subdue</u> with their great talent.

中譯　這十個人承諾會用他們的絕技制服姜子牙。

解析　Subdue 是及物動詞使服從、壓制的意思，後面必須帶受詞 Jiang Ziya。

KEY 60

They had set ten delicately designed formations with dangerous stratagems inside, planning to claim <u>as many lives as possible</u>.

They had set ten delicately designed formations with dangerous stratagems inside, planning to claim <u>many lives possible</u>.

中譯 他們佈下精心設計的十陣，十陣裡佈滿了危險機關，計畫儘可能的除掉許多人。

解析 As…as 修飾數量或程度，可以用 as much uncountable N as…或 as many countable N as…。

15-2 封神榜小故事｜ 🔘 *MP3 30*
異常凶險

Extremely dangerous

The Heaven Extinct Formation (天絕陣) smashes humans into ashes; the Ground Splitting Formation (地裂陣) swallows people into thunder and fire; the Wind Roaring Formation (風吼陣) produces destructive wind; and the Ice Block Formation (寒冰陣) freezes everyone inside. Besides, there were also six other formidable formations that kill people with light, fire, sand, blood, poison and spirit stealing.

The Ten Formations were extremely dangerous, Jiang Ziya almost lost his life in the Spirit Stealing Formation (落魂陣). Yao Bin (姚賓) the creator of the formation had made a straw man representing Jiang Ziya; then he pronounced a curse in order to deprive Jiang Ziya's spirit. Jiang Ziya back in Xiqi suddenly came down with a disease which had quickly deteriorated him. To save Jiang's life, Master Pure Essence (赤精子) snuck into the formation to take the straw man out.

Jiang Ziya called his teachers and fellow apprentices in the Chan Sect (闡教) to help break the formations. The Primeval Lord of Heaven had predicted the breaking of those formations would generate great sacrifice; however, the mandate of the heaven must be followed. During the ten formations cracking down, ten people had lost their lives. Their spirits all flew to the 'Investiture of Gods Platform'.

 異常凶險

天絕陣將人碾成粉末，地裂陣將人吞沒在雷與火中，風吼陣製造破壞力強的大風，寒冰陣將裡面的人凍結。除此之外，還有六個可怕的陣型，分別透過光、火、沙子、血、毒藥和偷取靈魂的方式殺人。

　　十陣非常凶險，姜子牙幾乎命喪落魂陣。陣主姚賓做了一個象徵姜子牙的稻草人，他每日唸咒以吸取姜子牙的靈魂。姜子牙回到西岐卻突然染上重病，並且迅速惡化。為了救姜子牙的命，赤精子道長潛入陣中偷走稻草人。

　　姜子牙號召他的闡教師兄師伯前來幫忙破陣。元始天尊算出破十陣會造成很大的犧牲，然而天命必須被遵從。在破十陣過程中，十個人失去了性命，他們的魂魄最後都飛入了封神台。

 「文法出題要點」

（　）1. The Heaven Extinct Formation _____ human into ashes.

（A）smash （B）smashes
（C）smashing （D）to smash

答　　案　　B

題目中譯　　天絕陣將人碾成粉末。

文法重點　　一般現在式第三人稱單數主詞的動詞型態

關鍵知識　　對十陣性質的描述是對客觀狀態對說明，用一般現在式。

文法解析　　「天絕陣」是一個單數名詞，因而動詞要加 S。單獨的動名詞和不定詞不可以做句子的動詞。

( ) 2. _____, there were also six other formidable formations that kill people with light, fire, sand, blood, poison and spirit stealing.

（A）Besides （B）Beside
（C）Be side （D）beside

答　案　A

題目中譯　除此之外，還有六個可怕的陣型，分別透過光、火、沙子、血、毒藥和偷取靈魂的方式殺人。

文法重點　Beside 和 besides。

關鍵知識　Besides 不是 beside 加 s 變出的派生字。

文法解析　Beside 是介系詞，表示在……旁邊、和……無關的意思。Besides 做介系詞，意思是除了……之外，besides做副詞時，意思是此外、而且。Besides 做副詞時放在句首，後面用逗點隔開。

( ) 3. Then he pronounced a curse _____ deprive Jiang Ziya's spirit.

（A）in order to （B）in order with
（C）in order that （D）so as that

答　案　A

| 題目中譯 | 他每日唸咒以吸取姜子牙的靈魂。 |

文法重點 In order to 的用法。

關鍵知識 In order to 和 so as to 都常用來表示目的，意思是：為了……。In order to 和 so as to 位置在句子中間時，也可以改寫為 in order that 和 so that 引導的副詞子句。

文法解析 In order to 後面接名詞，in order that 後面接句子。

（　）4. However, the mandate of the heaven must _____.

（A）following （B）follows
（C）follow （D）be followed

答　案 D

題目中譯 然而天命必須被遵從。

文法重點 情態動詞 must。

關鍵知識 情態動詞如 must, can, could, should, would 等，後面需要接原形動詞。

文法解析 此處的 must 後需要接被動語態，所以用原形 be＋過去分詞 followed。

楊戩

名詞、所有格、慣用語

16-1 封神榜小故事 | *MP3 31*
二郎神楊戩

Erlang Shen Yang Jian

Yang Jian was an apprentice of the Jade Tripod Immortal (玉頂真人) in Jade Spring Mountain. Yang Jian's mother was the younger sister of the Jade Emperor (玉皇大帝). She once got married with a mortal giving birth to a son named Yang Jian, which resulted in a violation of the rules as a goddess. So the Jade Emperor locked her up in the Peach Mountain for years as punishment. Yang Jian was half human and half deity; hence, he had superhuman strength. When he grew up, Yang Jian cleaved the entire mountain with an axe and saved his mother.

Yang Jian's weapon was the three-pointed, double-edged Lance (三尖兩刃刀). <u>This saber was so sharp that it could slice iron and steal as if they were mud.</u> Yang Jian wielded his lance with outstanding mastery and made himself one of the most powerful warriors in the Xiqi troop.

二郎神楊戩

楊戩是丅泉山玉頂真人的弟子。楊戩的母親是玉皇大帝的妹妹。她曾與凡人結婚並生下楊戩而觸犯天規，所以玉帝將她鎖在桃山數年作為懲罰。楊戩半人半神，力大無窮。他長大後，就用斧頭將整座山劈開救出了自己的母親。

楊戩使用三尖兩刃刀為兵器。這把刀削鐵如泥。楊戩有極高的用刀技巧，使得他成為西岐軍中最強的戰士之一。

文法正誤句

KEY 61

○ Yang Jian <u>was an apprentice</u> of the Jade Tripod Immortal in Jade Spring Mountain.

✗ Yang Jian <u>was an apprentices</u> of the Jade Tripod Immortal in Jade Spring Mountain.

楊戩是玉泉山玉頂真人的弟子。

解析 定冠詞 an 修飾單數名詞 apprentice；如果用複數名詞 apprentices，前面應當用 one of 來修飾。

🔥 KEY 62

○ Yang Jian's mother was <u>the younger sister of Jade Emperor</u>.

✗ Yang Jian's mother was <u>the younger sister of Jade Emperor's</u>.

中譯 楊戩的母親是玉皇大帝的妹妹。

解析 The sister of sb 已經是所有格，不需要在 Jade Emperor 後面加's 表示所有格。

🔥 KEY 63

○ So the Jade Emperor locked her up in the Peach Mountain for years <u>as punishment</u>.

✗ So the Jade Emperor locked her up in the Peach Mountain for years <u>as punish</u>.

中譯 所以玉帝將她鎖在桃山數年作為懲罰。

解析 介系詞 as 後面可以接名詞；如果接動詞的話，應當是動詞的 ing 形式而非原形。

KEY 64

This saber were so sharp that it could slice iron and steal <u>as if</u> they were mud.

~~This saber were so sharp that it could slice iron and steal <u>if as</u> they were mud.~~

中譯 這把刀削鐵如泥。

解析 As if 表示好像、似乎、彷彿，可以是陳述語氣，也可以是虛擬語氣。此處用作虛擬語氣。

16-2 封神榜小故事│ MP3 32
卓越的能力

Exceptional ability

In addition, Yang Jian possessed the skills of transforming himself into other things, a skill that is known as seventy-two transformation (七十二變). He also had a third eye on his forehead. This additional eye was able to distinguish truths from lies, and it possessed immense destructive power by generating energy blasts. Yang Jian's faithful pet the Howling Celestial Dog (哮天犬) followed him all the time offering support whenever he was fighting with villains. .

Erlang Shen Yang Jian's ultimate skill was the Eight Nine Divine Skill (八九玄功), which allowed Yang Jian's spirit to depart from his body temporarily, and provided him with invulnerability. Yang Jian was immune to all the attack as well as magical spells, so he could deal with any opponents. In addition, Yang Jian also possessed outstanding intelligence. He always came up with solutions at critical moments and saved Wu Wang's army multiple times.

卓越的能力

除此之外，楊戩還會七十二變。他額頭中間生了第三隻眼，這隻多出來的眼睛能夠分辨真偽，也可以釋放巨大能量因而擁有強大的破壞力。楊戩忠誠的寵物哮天犬時時刻刻跟著他，在攻擊惡人時提供助力。

二郎神楊戩的最高絕技是八九玄功，此功可以讓楊戩的靈魂暫時脫離軀體，使他不受侵害。楊戩不被攻擊和巫術所傷，所以他可以和任何對手對決。此外，楊戩還擁有過人的智慧，時常在關鍵時刻想出克敵良方，幾次拯救了武王的軍隊。

「文法出題要點」

（　）1. In addition, Yang Jian was capable _____ making
seventy-two transformations.

（A）in　　　　（B）on　　　　（C）of　　　　（D）to

答　　案	C
題目中譯	除此之外，楊戩還會七十二變。
文法重點	片語固定搭配。
關鍵知識	Be capable of＋動名詞，表示有能力做某事。
文法解析	Capable 固定搭配介系詞 of，不可以換作其他介詞。

（　）2. This additional eye was able to distinguish
truths _____ lies.

（A）from　　　　　　　（B）between
（C）and　　　　　　　（D）beside

答　　案	A
題目中譯	這隻多出來的眼睛能夠分辨真偽。
文法重點	Distinguish 的用法。
關鍵知識	Distinguish 的常用片語是 distinguish between a

and b 以及 distinguish a form b。

Distinguish between a and b 意在分出 a、b 之間的特質的差異；其中 between 是不能省略的，distinguish a and b 是錯誤用法。Distinguish a from b 不著重於區分 a 和 b 的差異性，意思是只要把 a 挑出來就可以。

( ) 3. Yang Jian's faithful pet the Howling Celestial Dog followed him all the time and _____ support whenever he was fighting with villains.

（A）offers （B）offered
（C）to offer （D）offering

答　案　D

題目中譯　楊戩忠誠的寵物哮天犬時時刻刻跟著他，在攻擊惡人時提供助力。

文法重點　動詞時態。

關鍵知識　整個句子有幾個並列關係的動詞，時態應當一致。

文法解析　Follow 和 play 都是哮天犬發出的動作，應當都是一般過去式。

（　）4. Erlang Shen Yang Jian's ultimate skill was the Eight Nine Divine Skill, which allowed Yang Jian's spirit _____ his body temporarily.

（A）leaves （B）to depart （C）leaving （D）left

答　案	B
題目中譯	二郎神楊戩的最高絕技是八九玄功，此功可以讓楊戩的靈魂暫時脫離軀體。
文法重點	Allow 的用法。
關鍵知識	Allow 的主要用法是 allow sb to do sth 和 allow doing sth。
文法解析	如果 allow 之後沒有直接接名詞，就用 allow doing，如 we don't allow smoking。如果 allow 之後接了名詞，就用 allow sb to do sth。

Unit 17

姜子牙戰勝趙公明

慣用語

17-1 封神榜小故事 | MP3 33
姜子牙戰勝趙公明

Jiang Ziya defeated Zhao Gongming／
姜子牙戰勝趙公明

The Grand Master Wen Zhong was disappointed with the failure of the ten formations. Wen Zhong went to the Kunlun Mountain to invite his good friend - the Taorist Hermit Zhao Gongming to join the war. Zhao Gongming was concerned that Zhou Wang was a hopeless despot; but for his friend Wen's sake, he still decided to support the increasingly declining Shang Dynasty for his friendship with Wen Zhong. Zhao Gongming visited his junior apprentice The Cloud Empress (雲霄娘娘) to borrow some magic weapons. The Cloud Empress was concerned about Zhao Gongming's choice because fighting Xiqi was against the will of heaven.

Zhao Gongming went to the frontline of Xiqi, riding his black tiger. He firstly requested to have a fight with Jiang Ziya. Within several rounds, Zhao used the whip, and the whip of Zhao Gongming beat Jiang Ziya to the ground. Zhao Gongming wielded the Dragon Constraint Chain (縛龍鎖) and the Ocean Setting Pearl (定海珠); he curbed all his opponents with the Chain and beat them badly with the Pearl.

 ## 姜子牙戰勝趙公明

聞太師對十陣的失敗感到非常失望。當他到崑崙山邀請自己的好友－道長趙公明來加入戰爭。趙公明顧慮到紂王是無道昏君，但他還是決定為了好友聞仲而支持日漸失勢的商朝。趙公明去找自己的師妹雲霞娘娘借法寶。雲霄娘娘對趙公明的選擇表示憂心，因為對抗西岐違反天意。

趙公明騎著他的黑虎來到對陣西岐的前線。他先要求姜子牙出戰，才幾個回合，趙公明就用鞭子把姜子牙打倒在地。趙公明施展縛龍鎖和定海珠，他將所有對手都用鎖鏈綑起來，並以定海珠痛打他們。

文法正誤句

KEY 65

〇 The Grand Master Wen Zhong was disappointed with the failure of the ten formations.

✕ The Grand Master Wen Zhong was disappointing with the failure of the ten formations.

中譯 聞太師對十陣的失敗感到非常失望。

解析 Disappointed 表示人感到失望，主詞是人；disappointing 表示事情令人失望，主詞是物。

KEY 66

〇 Zhao Gongming concerned that Zhou Wang was a hopeless despot.

✕ Zhao Gongming concerned that Zhou Wang was a helpless despot.

中譯 趙公明顧慮到紂王是無道昏君。

解析 Hopeless 表示沒有希望的、無可救藥的；helpless 則表示感到無助、無能為力的意思。

KEY 67

The Cloud Empress expressed her worries about Zhao Gongming's choice, <u>because</u> fighting Xiqi was against the will of heaven.

The Cloud expressed her worries about Zhao Gongming's choice <u>because of</u> fighting Xiqi was against the will of heaven.

中譯 雲霄娘娘對趙公明的選擇表示憂心，因為對抗西岐違反天意。

解析 Because 是一個連接詞，後面可以接一個句子；because of 是介系詞片語，後面只能接一個字或片語。

KEY 68

He curbed all his opponents with the Chain <u>and beat them badly</u> with the Pearl.

He curbed all his opponents with the Chain <u>and beated them badly</u> with the Pearl.

中譯 他將所有對手都用鎖鏈綑起來並以定海珠重傷。

解析 Beat 打的過去式也是 beat，過去分詞為 beaten。

A black magic

The magical power of Zhao Gongming was extremely powerful. No one in Xiqi was able to prevail against him. So Jiang Ziya sent Nezha, Leizhenzi, Yang Jian and Huang Tianhua to fight with Zhao Gongming jointly; four of them managed to force Zhao Gongming to retreat.

Taoist Master Lu Ya (陸壓道人) visited Jiang Ziya and told him the only way to beat Zhao Gongming would be fighting him indirectly. Jiang Ziya had no choice but to use a black magic. Following Lu Ya's instruction, Jiang Ziya built a soil platform and made an effigy of Zhao Gongming and prayed everyday with the spell force. Zhao Gongming was cursed to death on the twenty-first day after this black magic had started. Zhao Gongming later became the God of Wealth for his magic of turning stones into gold. Wen Zhong felt very sad and extremely guilty for Zhao Gonging's death. He was killed in the subsequent battle.

巫術

趙公明的法術非常強大。西岐幾乎沒有人可以贏過他。姜子牙於是派了哪吒、雷震子、楊戩和黃天化圍攻趙公明，四人聯手將他擊退。

陸壓道人找到姜子牙，告訴他只有用間接的方式才能贏過趙公明。姜子牙不得已只得採用了巫術。在陸壓的傳授下，姜子牙建了一個土台和趙公明的雕像，每天參拜唸咒。趙公明在巫術開始後的第二十一天因此死去。趙公明後來成了財神，因為他有點石成金的能力。趙公明的死令聞仲非常傷心和內疚，他在之後的戰鬥中也陣亡了。

「文法出題要點」

（　）1. No one in Xiqi was able to prevail _____ him.

（A）in　　　（B）against（C）on　　　（D）to

答　　案	B
題目中譯	西岐幾乎沒有人可以贏過他。
文法重點	片語固定搭配。
關鍵知識	Prevail 是不及物動詞，表示戰勝某人或流行。
文法解析	Prevail 的固定搭配是 prevail against/over sb。

（　）2. Taoist Master Lu Ya visited Jiang Ziya and told him the only way to win Zhao Gongming would be _____ him indirectly.

（A）fighting　　　　　（B）fight

（C）fights　　　　　（D）fought

答　　案	A
題目中譯	陸壓道人找到姜子牙，告訴他只有用間接的方式才能贏過趙公明。
文法重點	Be＋動名詞。
關鍵知識	Be 動詞之後要接動名詞形式。
文法解析	Be 之後不可以接原形動詞和過去式，這樣會造成一個句子裡兩個動詞。

（　）3. Jiang Ziya had no choice _____ use a black magic.

（A）and　　　　　（B）however

（C）but to　　　　　（D）but

答　　案	C
題目中譯	姜子牙不得已只得採用了巫術。
文法重點	不得不的一種用法。

關鍵知識 不得不的常用說法有 can't help but + 原形動詞，和 have no choice but to + 原形動詞。

文法解析 姜子牙 had no choice 後面不能接 however, and 或其他連接詞，接 but 時後面也應當加上 to 和原形動詞。

（　）4. Zhao Gongming later became the God of Wealth for his magic of _____ stones into gold.

（A）turn

（B）to turn

（C）turns

（D）turing

答　案 D

題目中譯 趙公明後來成了財神，因為他有點石成金的能力。

文法重點 介系詞後的動名詞。

關鍵知識 介系詞之後如果是接動詞，動詞要改寫為動名詞的形式。

文法解析 His magic of 後面要用 turning，不可以接原形動詞或不定詞。

鄧九公

主被動、時態、慣用語

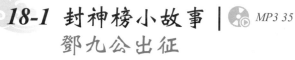

18-1 封神榜小故事 | MP3 35
鄧九公出征

Deng Jiugong's Expedition

After the death of Grand Master Wen Zhong, Zhou Wang sent Deng Jiugong, the General of the Three Mountains Pass (三山關), to continue the battle against Xiqi. Before the troop set off, Shen Gongbao recommended Tuxingsun (土行孫) to Deng Jiugong. Tuxingsun was a dwarf with an unattractive appearance. He was able to travel underground for several miles. Tuxingsun presented his treasure called the Immortal-binding Rope (捆仙繩). However, Deng Jiugong did not take Tuxingsun seriously.

When the two troops confronted one another, Deng Jiugong persuaded Jiang Ziya to surrender. Jiang Ziya replied loudly that Zhou Wang was a fatuous ruler and the Shang Dynasty was doomed to end. He suggested Deng Jiugong surrender and this infuriated Deng Jiugong. Deng Jiugong initiated a challenge, but Nezha injured Deng Jiugong's shoulder with the Universe Ring.

 ## 鄧九公出征

聞太師去世後，紂王派遣三山關總督鄧九公繼續與西岐作戰。大軍出發前，申公豹推薦了土行孫給鄧九公。土行孫是一個其貌不揚的矮個子。他能在地下穿行數哩。土行孫展示了叫做捆仙繩的寶物。不過鄧九公沒有把土行孫放在眼裡。

兩軍對陣後，鄧九公首先勸降姜子牙。姜子牙大聲回覆道：紂王昏庸，商朝注定要滅亡。姜子牙建議鄧九公投降西岐，這激怒了鄧九公。鄧九公發起挑戰，被哪吒用乾坤圈打傷了肩膀。

文法正誤句

KEY 69

○ After the death of Grand Master Wen Zhong, Zhou Wang sent Deng Jiugong, the General of the Three Mountains Pass, <u>to continue the battle</u> against Xiqi.

✗ After the death of Grand Master Wen Zhong, Zhou Wang sent Deng Jiugong, the General of the Three Mountains Pass, <u>continuing the battle</u> against Xiqi.

中譯 聞太師去世後，紂王派遣三山關總督鄧九公繼續與西岐作戰。

解析 To do sth 重點在於一次具體的行為，而 doing sth 則是側重於持續不斷的動作。

KEY 70

○ Tuxingsun was <u>a dwarf with unattractive appearance</u>.

✗ Tuxingsun was <u>a dwarf and unattractive appearance</u>.

中譯 土行孫是一個其貌不揚的矮個子。

解析 Unattractive appearance 是對 a dwarf 的修飾，二者

不是並列關係。

KEY 71

○ Tuxingsun presented <u>his treasure called</u> the Immortal-binding Rope.

✕ Tuxingsun presented <u>his treasure calling</u> the Immortal-binding Rope.

中譯 土行孫展示了叫做捆仙繩的寶物。

解析 Call 的過去分詞做形容詞，因為事物都是被命名的，有被動含義，因此用過去分詞而不是現在分詞。

KEY 72

○ Jiang Ziya replied loudly that <u>Zhou Wang was fatuous ruler and the Shang Dynasty was doomed to end.</u>

✕ Jiang Ziya replied loudly that <u>Zhou Wang is fatuous ruler and the Shang Dynasty is doomed to end.</u>

中譯 姜子牙大聲回覆道：紂王昏庸，商朝注定要滅亡。

解析 姜子牙說話的內容若放在引號中做直接引用，使用一般現在式；如果是沒有加引號的引述，就需要和主句時態一致，用一般過去式。

Earth-bounding power

At first, Nezha refused to have a fight with a maiden, requesting they changed to a general instead. However, Deng Chanyu suddenly released a Five-colored Stone and hit Nezha in his forehead. The stones were too quick to dodge. Deng Chanyu had hurt several Xiqi warriors until she was bit by Yang Jian's Howling Celestial Dog.

After Deng Chanyu fled back to the camp, Tuxingsun provided her with effective medicine and healed her wound. When Tuxingsun was having a battle with Nezha, Nezha could not hit Tuxingsun with the Universe Ring because Tuxingsun would dodge the attack by utilising the earth-bounding power to escape. Tuxingsun released the Immortal-binding Rope and captured Nezha. Deng Jiugong was extremely exhilarated by Tuxingsun's victory, promising that he will arrange the marriage between Tuxingsun and Deng Chanyu after they subdue Xiqi.

遁地術

一開始哪吒拒絕和小女孩，鄧嬋玉對戰，他要求對方換成將軍。但是鄧嬋玉突然丟出五色石，打傷了哪吒的額頭。石頭速度太快沒有時間躲開。鄧嬋玉打傷了幾員西岐大將，直到被楊戩的哮天犬咬傷。

鄧嬋玉逃回陣營後，土行孫拿出了有效的藥物醫好了鄧嬋玉的傷。當土行孫與哪吒交手時，哪吒根本無法用乾坤圈打中土行孫，因為他會施展遁地術逃走。土行孫放出捆仙繩把哪吒抓了起來。鄧九公對土行孫的勝利高興不已，他承諾征服西岐後會安排土行孫和鄧嬋玉結婚。

「文法出題要點」

（　）1. However, Deng Chanyu suddenly released a Five-colored Stone and hit Nezha _____ his forehead.

（A）in　　　（B）into　　　（C）on　　　（D）to

答　案　A

題目中譯　但是鄧嬋玉突然丟出五色石，打傷了哪吒的額頭。

文法重點　片語固定搭配。

關鍵知識　Hit 表示擊中、打中的意思時，慣用形式是 hit sb in ＋ 具體部位。

文法解析　Hit on 意思是突然想出好主意，如 I hit on an idea.
Hit 不搭配 into 和 to。

（　）2. Deng Chanyu _____ several Xiqi warriors until she was bit by Yang Jian's Howling Celestial Dog.

(A) hurt

(B) had hurt

(C) hurted

(D) hurts

答　案　B

題目中譯　鄧嬋玉打傷了幾員西岐大將，直到被楊戩的哮天犬咬傷。

文法重點　動詞時態。

關鍵知識　Hurt 的過去式和過去分詞都是 hurt。

文法解析　Hurted 是錯誤拼字，句子意思是鄧嬋玉被咬之前已經傷了多名大將，所以用過去完成式比一般過去式更貼切。

（　）3. After Deng Chanyu fled back to the camp, Tuxingsun provided _____ effective medicine and healed her wound.

(A) her for

(B) for

(C) with

(D) her with

| 答　　案 | D |

| 題目中譯 | 鄧嬋玉逃回陣營後，土行孫拿出了有效的藥物醫好了鄧嬋玉的傷。 |

| 文法重點 | Provide 的用法。 |

| 關鍵知識 | 及物動詞 provide 後面要緊跟一個受詞，provide sb with sth。 |

| 文法解析 | Provide 的另一種用法是 provide sth for sb。正確選型應當是 D。 |

（　）4. Nezha could ＿＿＿＿＿ hit Tuxingsun with the Universe Ring because Tuxingsun would dodge the attack by utilizing the earth-bounding power to escape.

（A）not　　　　　　　（B）never

（C）seldom　　　　　（D）suddenly

| 答　　案 | A |

| 題目中譯 | 哪吒根本無法用乾坤圈打中土行孫，因為他會施展遁地術逃走。 |

| 文法重點 | 根據上下文的意思作答。 |

| 關鍵知識 | 找到打中土行孫和土行孫會逃跑兩個句子的內在聯繫。 |

| 文法解析 | 句意為無法擊中，因而正確選項應當是 not。 |

土行孫

關係代名詞、不定詞、動詞

19-1 封神榜小故事 | MP3 37
收服土行孫

Surrender of Tuxingsun

During another battle, Jiang Ziya was bound by Tuxingsun's rope. He managed to escape before Tuxingsun captured him. Jiang Ziya had recognized the Immortal-binding Rope once belonged to Master Juliusun (懼留孫), who was also a disciple of the Primeval Lord of Heaven. Jiang Ziya could not believe Juliusun would fight against him. At the same time, Yang Jian reminded people to be aware of Tuxingsun's underground travel ability; so precautions must be taken to ensure Wu Wang's safety.

One night, Tuxingsun traveled underground into Xiqi city in order to assassinate Wu Wang. <u>He drilled out of Wu Wang's bedroom and killed Wu Wang while he was sleeping.</u> In fact, the Wu Wang in the bedroom was a stone in disguise, not the real one. It was a trick performed by Yang Jian and destroyed Tuxingsun's mission. Tuxingsun was captured by Yang Jian but once again he used earth-bound skill to escape.

 ## 收服土行孫

在另一場戰鬥中，姜子牙被土行孫捆了起來。他在被土行孫俘虜前逃了回去。姜子牙認出了捆仙繩是曾經屬於懼留孫的，懼留孫也是元始天尊的弟子。姜子牙不相信懼留孫會和自己作對。同時，楊戩提醒大家要提防土行孫的遁地術，要保衛好武王的安全。

一天晚上，土行為了暗殺武王遁地進入西岐城。他從武王的臥室鑽了出來，殺死了正在睡覺的武王。實際上，楊戩把一塊石頭變成了武王，破壞了土行孫的計劃。土行孫被楊戩抓了起來，不過他還是利用遁地術逃跑了。

文法正誤句

KEY 73

Jiang Ziya had identified the Immortal-binding Rope once belonged to Master Juliusun, <u>who was also a disciple</u> of the Primeval Lord of Heaven.

Jiang Ziya had identified the Immortal-binding Rope once belonged to Master Juliusun, <u>whom was also a disciple</u> of the Primeval Lord of Heaven.

中譯 姜子牙認出了捆仙繩是曾經屬於懼留孫的，懼留孫也是元始天尊的弟子。

解析 關係代名詞做子句的主詞，不可以用受格。

KEY 74

Jiang Ziya could not <u>believe Juliusun would fight against him.</u>

Jiang Ziya could not <u>believe in Juliusun would fight against him.</u>

中譯 姜子牙不相信懼留孫會和自己作對。

解析　Believe 表示相信，後面可以接一個子句；believe in 表示信仰、…有信心，后面接單字或片語 。

KEY 75

Yang Jian reminded people <u>to be aware of</u> Tuxingsun's underground travel ability.

Yang Jian reminded people <u>to aware of</u> Tuxingsun's underground travel ability.

中譯　楊戩提醒大家要提防土行的遁地術。

解析　Aware 是一個形容 ，必須用在 be aware of 片語中。

KEY 76

He drilled out of Wu Wang's bedroom and <u>killed Wu Wang while he was sleeping</u>.

He drilled out of Wu Wang's bedroom and <u>killed Wu Wang while he slept</u>.

中譯　他從武王的臥室鑽了出來，殺死了正在睡覺的武王。

解析　依while引導的子句中，時態要用過去進行式，故為was sleeping。

Juliusun

Yang Jian visited Juliusun in the Flying Dragon Cave to find out what was going on. Juliusun found out his Immortal-binding Rope was stolen by his apprentice Tuxingsun; so he followed Yang Jian to Jiang Ziya's camp.

The next time Tuxingsun released the rope, Juliusun showed up and collected it. Before Tuxingsun managed to flee, Juliusun turned the ground under Tuxingsun into iron. Tuxingsun bumped his head during the ground-drilling effort. Then he was bound by the rope and captured to the Xiqi camp. Tuxingsun admitted that Shen Gongbao instigated him to commit the evil acts. He surrendered to Jiang Ziya and made a pledge to serve Xiqi. Juliusun forgave his disciple and returned to the Flying Dragon Cave. Tuxingsun was left in Xiqi to assist Jiang Ziya.

懼留孫

　　楊戩去飛龍洞訪問懼留孫，來弄清事情的原委。懼留孫發現他的捆仙繩被徒弟土行孫偷走了，所以跟著楊戩回到了西岐營中。

　　土行孫再次使用捆仙繩的時候，捆仙繩就被懼留孫收了回去。在土行孫逃跑前，懼留孫把土行孫身下的地面變成了鐵。土行孫努力遁地時撞壞了自己的頭，被捆仙繩捉起來押回了西岐。土行孫承認是申公豹教唆他做出這些惡行。他想向姜子牙投降並承諾效忠西岐。懼留孫原諒了徒弟並返回了飛龍洞，將土行孫留在西岐軍中協助姜子牙。

「文法出題要點」

（　）1. Yang Jian visited Juliusun in the Flying Dragon Cave _____ what was going on.

（A）finds out 　　　　（B）find out

（C）finding out 　　　（D）to find out

答　案	D
題目中譯	楊戩去飛龍洞訪問懼留孫，來弄清事情的原委。
文法重點	不定詞表目的
關鍵知識	不定詞做目的狀語修飾動詞，表示「為了……」。
文法解析	楊戩造訪飛龍洞的目的是找到土行孫事件的真相，應當

用不定詞。

（　）2. Juliusun found out his Immortal-binding Rope was _____ by his apprentice Tuxingsun.

（A）stole （B）stealed
（C）steal （D）stolen

答　　案　　D

題目中譯　懼留孫發現他的捆仙繩被徒弟土行孫偷走了。

文法重點　動詞時態。

關鍵知識　Steal 的過去式是 stole，過去分詞是 stolen。

文法解析　捆仙繩是被偷走，所以用表被動態的 be＋過去分詞。

（　）3. _____ Tuxingsun managed to flee, Juliusun turned the ground under Tuxingsun into iron.

（A）After （B）Before
（C）Since （D）If

答　　案　　B

題目中譯　在土行孫逃跑前，懼留孫把土行孫身下的地面變成了鐵。

| 文法重點 | 表示時間先後的連接詞。 |

文法重點　表示時間先後的連接詞。

關鍵知識　Before 可以做介系詞、連接詞和副詞。

文法解析　因為要在土行孫逃跑之前就把地面變成鐵，所以應當選擇連接詞 before。

（　）4. Tuxingsun admitted that Shen Gongbao taught him to ＿＿＿＿＿＿ the evil acts.

（A）happen　　　　　（B）commit
（C）make　　　　　（D）take

答　案　B

題目中譯　土行孫承認是申公豹教唆他做出這些惡行。

文法重點　犯罪的動詞。

關鍵知識　Commit 常接 crime, murder, offence 等表示犯罪的字彙。

文法解析　Evil acts 搭配的動詞是 commit，表示犯下罪行的意思。

20-1 封神榜小故事 | MP3 39
蘇護討伐西岐

Su Hu led force to Xiqi

Jiang Ziya sent a messenger to Deng Jiugong's army, bringing the message that Tuxingsun had already surrendered to Xiqi. In addition, the messenger made a formal proposal of engagement between Tuxingsun and Deng Chanyu. Deng Jiugong said it was a promise made while he was drunk. He had already regretted to marry his daughter to Tuxingsun. But one of Deng Jiugong's subordinates suggested that he accept the proposal as a pretence; they could then invite Jiang Ziya to their camp and capture him.

After the messenger returned, both sides had secretly planned a sudden attack on each other. <u>Jiang Ziya had foreseen Deng Jiugong's plot, so he made a more meticulous plan.</u> During Jiang Ziya's visit, the Xiqi force abducted Deng Chanyu. Deng Chanyu was truly moved by Tuxingsun and they held the marriage. Missing his daughter too much, Deng Jiugong also came over to Jiang Ziya's side.

 ## 蘇護討伐西岐

姜子牙派了使者去鄧九公的軍中，帶去了土行孫已經投降西岐的消息。使者還帶去了為土行孫和鄧嬋玉訂婚的正式請求。鄧九公說他的承諾是酒醉時作出的，他已經後悔了。但是鄧九公的一個下屬建議他先假裝接受對方的請求，再邀請姜子牙來營中把他抓起來。

信使回去後，兩邊都開始秘密策劃攻擊對方。姜子牙預測到鄧九公的陰謀，所以做了更精心的準備。西岐軍在姜子牙拜訪商朝軍營時綁架了鄧嬋玉。土行孫用真心打動了鄧嬋玉，兩人便結了婚。鄧九公由於太過思念女兒，也加入了姜子牙的陣營。

文法正誤句

KEY 77

Jiang Ziya sent a messenger to Deng Jiugong's army, brought the message <u>that Tuxingsun had already surrendered</u> to Xiqi.

Jiang Ziya sent a messenger to Deng Jiugong's army, brought the message <u>that Tuxingsun has already surrendered</u> to Xiqi.

中譯 姜子牙派了使者去鄧九公的軍中，帶去了土行孫已經投降西岐德消息。

解析 派使者的行為是過去式，因此帶去的消息應當是過去完成式。

KEY 78

Deng Jiugong said it was a promise made <u>while he was drunk.</u>

Deng Jiugong said it was a promise made <u>during he was drunk.</u>

中譯 鄧九公說他的承諾是酒醉時作出的。

解析 依句意要用while而非during。

KEY 79

○ But one of Deng Jiugong's subordinates <u>suggested that he should</u> accept the proposal as a pretence.

✗ But one of Deng Jiugong's subordinates <u>suggested him accepting</u> the proposal as a pretence.

中譯 但是鄧九公的一個下屬建議他先假裝接受對方的請求。

解析 Suggest 的用法有 suggest that sb (should) + 動詞，和 suggest +動名詞。Suggest＋Ving 形式中間不能加入其他詞字。

KEY 80

○ Jiang Ziya had foreseen Deng Jiugong's plot, so <u>he made</u> a more meticulous plan.

✗ Jiang Ziya had foreseen Deng Jiugong's plot, so he makes a more meticulous plan.

中譯 姜子牙預測到鄧九公的陰謀，所以做了更精心的準備。

解析 姜子牙做了更精心的準備，是過去發生的事實，故要用過去式。

163

Deng Jiugong's betrayal

Zhou Wang was angry about Deng Jiugong's betrayal, so he sent Daji's father Su Hu to conquer Xiqi. Zhou Wang believed Su Hu must be more faithful to him since Su Hu is a relative with the royal family. But actually Su Hu had no intention of fighting with Xiqi. He also planned to join Wu Wang's troop as soon as possible.

Su Hu captured several Xiqi Soldiers, but he set them free. He asked those soldiers to send Wu Wang a message. Su Hu told the soldiers that he yearned to join Xiqi. Su Hu wished to arrange a secret meeting with Jiang Ziya the following evening. However, on the next day, a Taorist Priest visited Su Hu in the camp, the priest said he was Lu Yue (呂岳) from the Nine Dragons Island, he came to assist Su Hu to fight Xiqi.

 ## 鄧九公的背叛

紂王對鄧九公的背叛非常憤怒，所以派遣妲己的父親蘇護出征西岐。紂王認為蘇護是皇親國戚，一定對他忠心。但實際上蘇護根本不

想和西岐對抗，他想要儘快加入武王的軍隊。

蘇護俘獲了幾名西岐士兵，釋放他們時蘇護請士兵們向武王傳話。蘇護說他早就盼望可以效力西岐。蘇護想約定第二天晚上密會姜子牙。但是就在第二天，一個道長拜訪蘇護的軍營，他說自己是九龍島的呂岳，特地趕來幫助蘇護和西岐對抗。

「文法出題要點」

（　）1. Zhou Wang was angry ＿＿＿＿＿ Deng Jiugong's betrayal.

　　　（A）of　　　（B）about　　（C）with　　　（D）at

答　案　B

題目中譯　紂王對鄧九公的背叛非常憤怒。

文法重點　Be angry 的用法

關鍵知識　動詞 angry 後面接不同的介系詞，意義上有微小的差別。be angry at＋事物，在事發的當下，對……感到氣憤；be angry with＋人，生某人的氣；be angry about＋事物，事情發生後一段時間，對……感到氣憤。

文法解析　鄧九公背叛是之前發生的事，所以選擇 about。

（　）2. But actually Su Hu had no intention _____ with Xiqi.

（A）fight　　　　　　　（B）fighting

（C）fights　　　　　　（D）of fighting

答　案　D

題目中譯　但實際上蘇護根本不想和西岐對抗。

文法重點　Intention 的用法。

關鍵知識　名詞 intention 後面經常接 to+原形動詞或 of+動名詞。

文法解析　可以說 no intention to fight 或 no intention of fighting。

（　）3. Su Hu told the soldiers that he _____ to join Xiqi.

（A）lusted　　　　　　（B）eager

（C）coveted　　　　　（D）yearned

答　案　D

題目中譯　蘇護說他早就盼望可以效力西岐。

文法重點　動詞的感情色彩。

關鍵知識　Yearn 是渴望的意思。

| 文法解析 | Eager 是一個形容詞，lust 和 covet 都有負面的含義。 |

( ) 4. _____, on the next day, a Taorist Priest visited Su Hu in the camp.

　　（A）However 　　　　　（B）Furthermore
　　（C）In addition 　　　　（D）Moreover

答　　案	A
題目中譯	但是就在第二天，一個道長來到蘇護的軍營。
文法重點	連接詞的選擇。
關鍵知識	However 為表轉折關係的副詞連接詞。
文法解析	呂岳的到來打亂了蘇護投降的計劃，所以應當用轉折意義的連接詞。Furthermore, moreover 和 in addition 是表示遞進關係的連接詞。

Unit 21

楊戩

名詞、時態、定冠詞

21-1 封神榜小故事 | MP3 41
西岐瘟疫

The plague in Xiqi

Lu Yue took four of his disciples to the battle. These disciples were all experts in cult and poison. After fighting with Lu Yue's disciple, Jinzha suffered from an unbearable headache, Muzha was seriously burnt, Leizhenzi wounded his wings and fell from sky, and the Dragon Beard Tiger was poisoned. The wounded Xiqi warriors were all infected with plague and became extremely weak.

During the battle, the figure of Lu Yue developed into three heads and six arms, putting massive pressure on the Xiqi army. Nezha, Yang Jian, Tuxingsun, Huang

Tianhua and Jiang Ziya formed a circle to fight Lu Yue together. Lu Yue could not beat rivals who outnumbered him and he ran away in a hurry.

Lu Yue ordered his disciples to poison every river and well in Xiqi city making the entire population infect with plague. Soon after, all the other people except lotus incarnated Nezha and half deity Yang Jian, were all infected with the plague.

西岐瘟疫

呂岳帶了他的四個弟子來作戰。這幾個弟子都擅長使用旁門左道。跟呂岳的徒弟過招後，金吒頭痛難忍、木吒被嚴重燒傷，雷震子翅膀受傷從天上摔下來，龍鬚虎中毒。受傷的西岐戰士都感染了瘟疫，變得格外虛弱。

呂岳在打鬥時長出三頭六臂，令西岐軍大感壓力。哪吒、楊戩、土行孫、黃天化和姜子牙圍攻呂岳。呂岳寡不敵眾，匆匆逃走。

呂岳命令徒弟在西岐所有的河內、井內投毒，讓全城的人都感染了瘟疫。不久，除了蓮花化身的哪吒和半仙的楊戩，其他所有人都感染了瘟疫。

文法正誤句

KEY 81

○ These disciples <u>were all experts</u> in cult and poison.

✕ These disciples <u>were all expert</u> in cult and poison.

中譯 這幾個弟子都擅長使用旁門左道。

解析 Experts 和 disciples 相對應，都應該是複數名詞。

KEY 82

○ Leizhenzi wounded his wings and <u>fell form sky.</u>

✕ Leizhenzi wounded his wings and <u>falled form sky.</u>

中譯 雷震子翅膀受傷從天上摔下來。

解析 Fall 為不規則動詞，過去式是 fell，過去分詞是 fallen。

KEY 83

○ During the battle, the figure of Lu Yue three heads and six arms, <u>posing massive pressure</u> to Xiqi army.

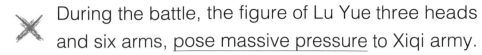

During the battle, the figure of Lu Yue three heads and six arms, <u>pose massive pressure</u> to Xiqi army.

中譯 呂岳在打鬥時長出三頭六臂，令西岐軍大感壓力。

解析 分詞構句是從副詞子句或對等子句轉化而來，做句子修飾語，表示原因、條件、讓步等修飾關係。分詞構句的結構為現在分詞／過去分詞……，主句。

KEY 84

Lu Yue ordered his disciples to poison <u>every river</u> and well in Xiqi city, making the entire population infect with plague.

Lu Yue ordered his disciples to poison <u>every rivers and wells</u> in Xiqi city making the entire population infect with plague.

中譯 呂岳命令徒弟在西岐所有的河內井內投毒，讓全城的人都感染了瘟疫。

解析 Every 修飾的名詞應當都是單數名詞。

Seeking for a cure

At this crucial moment, Su Hu's assistant general Zheng Lun (鄭倫) led the Shang army to attack the Xiqi City. People were too sick to defend the city, so Yang Jian sprinkled lots of grass seeds on the top of city's defensive wall. The seeds turned into giant men patrolling the city, scaring away Zheng Lun's army.

Yang Jian struggled to find a cure for all the sick people. Luckily, his teacher the Jade Tripod Immortal came to Xiqi in time. The Immortal told Yang Jian to make his way to the Fire Cloud Pit (火雲洞), and take medicine from the Three Sages (三聖). Yang Jian immediately went to the Fire Cloud Pit and brought back antidotes. After his return, Yang Jian dissolved the pills in water, and sprinkled the water all over the city with a willow branch. Not long after, everyone recovered. The Xiqi army made a devastating strike, and Lu Yue fled back to the Nine Dragons Island.

尋求解藥

在這個危機時刻，蘇護的副將鄭倫帶領商軍進攻西岐。人們病得無力保護城市，於是楊戩把草籽灑在西岐城牆上，草籽變成了大漢在城牆上巡邏，嚇退了鄭倫的軍隊。

楊戩窮盡心力想要解救所有病人。幸運的是他的師父玉頂真人及時來到西岐，真人告訴楊戩應該去火雲洞三聖大師那裡尋求解藥。楊戩馬上去了火雲洞帶了解藥回來。他把藥溶在水裡，用柳條將水灑遍了西岐全城。不久後，所有人就康復了。西岐軍做了有力回擊，呂岳逃回了九龍島。

「文法出題要點」

（　）1. At this crucial moment, Su Hu's assistant general Zheng Lun _____ the Shang army to attack the Xiqi City.

（A）lead （B）leaded

（C）leading （D）led

答　　案　D

題目中譯　在這個危機時刻，蘇護的副將鄭倫帶領商軍進攻西岐。

文法重點　Lead 的時態

Lead 過去式和過去分詞為 led。

鄭倫進攻西岐的行為發生在過去,用一般過去式。

( ) 2. The seeds turned into giant men _____ the city.

（A）to patrol （B）patrols

（C）patrol （D）patrolling

D

草籽變成了大漢在城牆上巡邏。

現在分詞做受詞補語。

Ing 形式的動詞有時是現在分詞,有時是動名詞。區分兩者的方法是:動名詞主要是名詞功用,在一個句子中,動名詞時常做句子的主詞、或一般動詞的受詞、或介系詞的受詞。現在分詞主要是形容詞功用,做修飾語或補語。

選項 A 動詞不定詞主要表示目的,而這個句子主要是描述狀態。B 和 C 也不能作為正確選擇,因為一個句子中只能有一個動詞。

( ) 3. The Immortal told Yang Jian to _____ to the Fire Cloud Pit, and take medicine form the Three Sages.

（A）make its way　　（B）make he way

（C）make him way　　（D）make his way

| 答　案 | D |

| 題目中譯 | 真人告訴楊戩應該去火雲洞三聖大師那裡尋求解藥。 |

| 文法重點 | 片語 make one's way。 |

| 關鍵知識 | Make one's way 表示向前走，或取得成功的意思。 |

| 文法解析 | Make 和 way 之間應該是代詞或名詞的所有格。 |

（　）4. After he returned, Yang Jian dissolved the pills in water, and sprinkled ＿＿＿＿＿ all over the city with a willow branch.

（A）this water　　（B）waters

（C）water　　　　（D）the water

| 答　案 | D |

| 題目中譯 | 他把藥溶在水裡，用柳條灑將水灑遍了西岐全城。 |

| 文法重點 | 定冠詞 the 的用法。 |

| 關鍵知識 | The 用於指出特定名詞或前述名詞。 |

| 文法解析 | 前文有說到 dissolved the pills in water，所以再次提到 water 時就是特指，應當加上定冠詞 the。 |

殷洪

慣用語、名詞子句、副詞連接詞

22-1 封神榜小故事 | MP3 43
殷洪的宿命

Yin Hong met his doom

Daji once set a conspiracy and killed the Queen Jiang (姜皇后) - the mother of Prince Yin Jiao (殷郊) and Prince Yin Hong (殷洪). Two princes were so enraged that they rushed into the palace and tried to kill Daji. <u>Zhou Wang sentenced both of his sons to death</u>; and the siblings were forced to escape.

Yin Hong was saved and trained by Pure Essence. One day, Pure Essence gave Yin Hong all his magic weapons. <u>He told Yin Hong that the time for revenge had came</u> Yin Hong was asked to join Jiang Ziya's army and aid them to overthrow the Shang Dynasty. However, Pure Essence had misgivings about Yin Hong's loyalty to Xiqi, making him vow that he will be faithful to Wu Wang.

On the way to join Xiqi, Yin Hong met Shen Gongbao. Shen Gongbao laughed at Yin Hong's choice, convincing him to switch back to his father's side. Yin Hong ended up joining Su Hu's troop after conversing with Shen Gongbao.

殷洪的宿命

妲己曾經設下陰謀害死了姜皇后——太子殷郊和王子殷洪的母親。兩位皇子憤怒的衝入宮中要殺妲己。紂王下令處死兩個兒子，兩兄弟只得逃跑。

殷洪被赤精子所救並收在門下修行。有一天，赤精子將自己所有法寶交給了殷洪。他告訴殷洪報仇的時機已到，派他前去姜子牙軍中協助攻擊商朝都城。不過赤精子也顧慮到殷洪對西岐的忠誠度，就讓殷洪用性命發誓要忠於武王。

在前往西岐的路上，殷洪遇到了申公豹。申公豹嘲笑了殷洪的選擇，並說服了殷洪回去為他的父親效力。和申公豹談話後，殷洪就去了蘇護的軍營。

文法正誤句

KEY 85

 Zhou Wang <u>sentenced both of his sons to death</u>.

 Zhou Wang <u>sentenced both of his sons to die</u>.

中譯 紂王下令處死兩個兒子。

解析 處死某人的固定用法是 sentence sb to death。

KEY 86

 <u>He told Yin Hong that</u> the time for revenge had came.

 <u>He told Yin Hong this</u> the time for revenge had came.

中譯 他告訴殷洪報仇的時機已到。

解析 That＋名詞子句，that 做可以省略的連接詞。This 沒有這個功用。

KEY 87

 <u>However</u>, Pure Essence had misgivings about Yin Hong's loyalty to Xiqi.

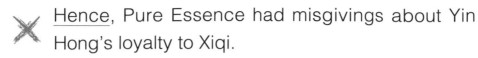

Hence, Pure Essence had misgivings about Yin Hong's loyalty to Xiqi.

中譯 然而，赤精子也顧慮到殷洪對西岐的忠誠度。

解析 此處要用的是轉折關係的副詞連接詞，不是因果關係的副詞連接詞。

KEY 88

Shen Gongbao laughed at Yin Hong's choice and convinced him to switch back to his father's side.

Shen Gongbao was laughed at Yin Hong's choice and convinced him to switch back to his father's side.

中譯 申公豹嘲笑了殷洪的選擇，並說服了殷洪回去為他的父親效力。

解析 申公豹發出了嘲笑這個動作，是主動語態，如果是 be laughed at 就變成了被動語態。

Taoist Master Merciful Navigation brought an atlas

During the fight, Yin Hong captured Huang Feihu and his clan. Since Huang Feihu once saved him from Zhou Wang's chasing; Yin Hong released Huang Feihu to reciprocate his favor. With the help of his master's magical weapons, Yin Hong became really powerful. Pure Essence was angry after knowing Yin Hong had joined Su Hu's side. He arrived at the frontline to deal with Yin Hong. Pure Essence rebuked Yin Hong for his betrayal, but Yin Hong wielded all the magic weapons and defeated his teacher with all the magic weapons.

On the next battle, Taoist Master Merciful Navigation brought an atlas to Xiqi. After Jiang Ziya unfolded the map onto the ground, a golden bridge appeared. Jiang Ziya led Yin Hong on the bridge. When Pure Essence folded the map up, Yin Hong turned into ashes. Pure Essence emptied over killing his own disciple, but he had no other choice. After Yin Hong's death, Su Hu finally managed to join Wu Wang's army.

慈航道人帶來了一幅地圖

　　在戰鬥中，殷洪俘虜了黃飛虎一家。因為黃飛虎曾在殷洪被紂王追殺時救過他，為了報答他的救命恩情，殷洪釋放了黃飛虎。借助他師傅的法寶的威力，殷洪變得非常強大。赤精子聽說殷洪加入蘇護大軍後非常生氣，他來到兩軍對陣的前線找殷洪。赤精子怒斥殷洪的背叛，但殷洪用法寶把他的老師打跑了。

　　在下一次對戰時，慈航道人給西岐帶來了一幅地圖。姜子牙把地圖在地上展開後，就出現了一座金橋出現。姜子牙將殷洪引到橋上，赤精子將圖捲起來，殷洪就化作了灰。赤精子因為殺死了自己的徒弟難過地哭泣，但是他沒得選擇。殷洪死後，蘇護終於如願可以加入武王大軍。

「文法出題要點」

（　）1. Yin Hong released Huang Feihu to _____ his favor.

（A）debt （B）reciprocate
（C）award （D）price

答　　案	B
題目中譯	作為報答殷洪釋放了黃飛虎。

(　) 2. _____ the help of his master's magical weapons, Yin Hong became really powerful.

（A）Since 　　（B）With 　　（C）At 　　（D）Of

答　　案　B

題目中譯　借助他師傅的法寶的威力，殷洪變得非常強大。

文法重點　介詞片語固定搭配。

關鍵知識　With the help of 表示在……的幫助下。

文法解析　借助……的幫助也可以搭配其他介系詞，如 under the help of，by the help of 等。

(　) 3. Pure Essence scolded Yin Hong for his _____, but Yin Hong wielded all the magic weapons and defeated his teacher away.

（A）betrays 　　　　　（B）betray

（C）betrayal 　　　　　（D）betrayed

答　　案	C
題目中譯	赤精子怒斥殷洪的背叛，但殷洪用法寶把他的老師打跑了。
文法重點	介系詞後加名詞。
關鍵知識	介系詞之後只能接名詞或動名詞。
文法解析	Betrayal 是一個名詞，其他選項都是動詞的各種時態變形。

（　）4. After Jiang Ziya threw the map on ground, a golden bridge ＿＿＿＿＿＿.

　　（A）appearing 　　（B）appears

　　（C）appear 　　（D）appeared

答　　案	D
題目中譯	姜子牙把地圖在地上展開，就有一座金橋出現。
文法重點	動詞的時態。
關鍵知識	After 引導時間副詞子句是過去式，主句也應當是過去式。
文法解析	D 選項 appeared 是過去式，為正確選項。

Unit 23

殷郊的背叛

慣用語、條件句、複數名詞

23-1 封神榜小故事 | MP3 45
殷郊的背叛

Yin Jiao's Revolt

Grand Completion (廣成子) heard the news that Jiang Ziya needed support to attack the Shang Dynasty. He sent his apprentice Prince Yin Jiao to aid Jiang Ziya. Yin Jiao granted Grand Completion's Heaven Revolving Seal (翻天印) and Spirit Dropping Bell (落魂鐘), and started off for Xiqi.

Shen Gongbao found Yin Jiao before he arrived at Xiqi. He told Yin Jiao that Jiang Ziya would never trust Shang descendants; and Yin Hong was killed by Jiang Ziya not long after. Prince Yin Jiao felt resentful and decided to support Shang instead.

Grand Completion's weapons were extremely powerful. Yin Jiao injured Nezha with the Heaven Revolving Seal. He also made Huang Tianhua fall from his unicorn by ringing the Spirit Dropping Bell. When he tried to attack Jiang Ziya with the Seal again, Jiang Ziya waved his apricot coloured flag as a shield intercepting the seal on the outside.

 ## 殷郊的背叛

廣成子得到姜子牙討伐商紂需要幫助的消息，他就派了自己的弟子殷郊去協助姜子牙。殷郊得到了廣成子的法寶翻天印和落魂鐘，向西岐出發。

申公豹在他到達西岐前攔住了殷郊。他告訴殷郊姜子牙絕對不會信任殷商後裔，殷洪不久前就被姜子牙殺死了。太子殷郊感到非常憤恨，決定轉而支持商朝。

廣成子的寶物極為強大。殷郊用翻天印打傷了哪吒，他又搖動落魂鐘讓黃天化從麒麟上跌落。殷郊再用翻天印打姜子牙時，姜子牙揮舞杏黃旗當盾牌，把印擋在外面。

文法正誤句

KEY 89

○ Yin Jiao granted Grand Completion's Heaven Revolving Seal and Spirit Dropping Bell, <u>and started off</u> to Xiqi.

✗ Yin Jiao granted Grand Completion's Heaven Revolving Seal and Spirit Dropping Bell, <u>and started from</u> to Xiqi.

中譯 殷郊得到了廣成子的法寶翻天印和落魂鐘，向西岐出發。

解析 Start off 是動詞片語表示出發、開始。

KEY 90

○ He told Yin Jiao that Jiang Ziya <u>would never trust</u> the Shang descendants.

✗ He told Yin Jiao that Jiang Ziya <u>should never trust</u> the Shang descendants.

中譯 他告訴殷郊姜子牙絕對不會信任殷商後裔。

解析 Would 用於條件句，通常表示不會或沒有發生的情況。Should 是 shall 的過去式，意思是應該。

KEY 91

○ Grand Completion's <u>weapons were</u> extremely powerful.

✗ Grand Completion's <u>weapon were</u> extremely powerful.

中譯 廣成子的寶物極為強大。

解析 Weapons 複數名詞接動詞 were，如果是單數形式 weapon 應當接動詞 was。

KEY 92

○ He also <u>made Huang Tianhua fall</u> from his unicorn by ringing the Spirit Dropping Bell.

✗ He also <u>made Huang Tianhua fell</u> from his unicorn by ringing the Spirit Dropping Bell.

中譯 他又搖動落魂鐘讓黃天化從麒麟上跌落。

解析 使某人做某事 make sb do sth，動詞要用原形。

Four magical flags

Yang Jian informed Grand Completion of Yin Jiao's treachery, but Grand Completion had already given out all his weapons to Yin Jiao, making the master unable to control his disciple anymore. Master Burning Lamp suggested that more flags be prepared to obstruct Yin Jiao's Heaven Revolving Seal. Grand Completion borrowed the Fire-flame Flag (火焰旗), the Immortal-gathering Flag (聚仙旗), and the Green Lotus Flag (青蓮旗) from other deities, planning to hunt Yin Jiao down.

After a huge battle took place, Yin Jiao was trapped by the four magical flags, so he could not utilize the Seal to hurt anyone. Yin Jiao rushed away with his treasury weapons, but his way was blocked by a giant mountain. To escape, Yin Jiao split the mountain with the seal and ran into the crack. Master Burning Lamp closed the mountain together. Yin Jiao got nipped into the mountain and lost his life.

四面旗子

　　楊戩向廣成子告知了殷郊的背叛。但廣成子已經把所有法寶傳給了殷郊，所以已經無法控制徒弟了。燃燈道人建議要準備更多的旗擋住翻天印。廣成子就向其他神仙借來了火焰旗、聚仙旗和青蓮旗，準備制服殷郊。

　　大戰開始，殷郊被四面旗子封住，所以無法施展出翻天印傷人。殷郊急忙帶著寶物逃跑，卻被大山攔住去路。為了逃跑，殷郊用印劈開大山並衝入裂縫中。燃燈道人合攏了大山，殷郊就被大山夾住丟了性命。

 「**文法出題要點**」

（　　）1. Yang Jian informed Grand Completion _____ Yin Jiao's treachery.

　　　　（A）to　　　（B）of　　　（C）about　　（D）for

答　　案	B
題目中譯	楊戩向廣成子告知了殷郊的背叛。
文法重點	把某事告訴某人的說法。
關鍵知識	把某事告訴某人，通知某人某事常用 inform sb of sth。

189

Inform sb of sth 也可以說成 tell sb of sth，一般不用 inform sb about sth，inform sb about 後面可以接一個字句。

（　）2. Master Burning Lamp suggested that more flags _____ to obstruct Yin Jiao's Heaven Revolving Seal.

（A）preparing　　　（B）prepared

（C）prepare　　　　（D）be prepared

答　案 D

題目中譯 燃燈道人建議要準備更多的旗擋住翻天印。

文法重點 Suggest 的用法。

關鍵知識 Suggest 的慣常用法是 suggest that S (should) V+子句，或 suggest +動名詞。

文法解析 旗子是被準備的，要用被動語態。由於句子裡有省略的 should，動詞部分應當是 be prepared。

（　）3. Yin Jiao rushed away with his treasury weapons, but his way was blocked _____ a giant mountain.

（A）to 　　　　　　　　（B）out
（C）by 　　　　　　　　（D）from

答　　案	C
題目中譯	殷郊急忙帶著寶物逃跑，卻被大山攔住去路。
文法重點	介系詞的選擇。
關鍵知識	被某物體阻攔是固定搭配 block by。
文法解析	Block out 也是阻隔、阻攔的意思，但應當用於主動語態。

（　）4. To escape, Yin Jiao ＿＿＿＿＿＿ the mountain with the seal and ran into the crack.

（A）was split 　　　　　（B）splitting
（C）splits 　　　　　　　（D）split

答　　案	D
題目中譯	為了逃跑，殷郊用印劈開大山並衝入裂縫中。
文法重點	動詞的時態。
關鍵知識	Split 的過去式和過去分詞還是 split。
文法解析	被動態和一般現在式都不能做為正確選項。

姜子牙

慣用語、不定詞、副詞

24-1 封神榜小故事 | 🎧 *MP3 47*
孔雀製造的麻煩

Trouble caused by a peacock

Zhou Wang sent more men to attack Xiqi, but none had returned with victory. On the other hand, Jiang Ziya persuaded Wu Wang that they should initiate attacks to overthrow the fatuous Zhou Wang and save people from suffering. Wu Wang appointed Jiang Ziya as the general commander and ordered the Xiqi army to head east.

At the Golden Rooster Ridge (金雞嶺), the Xiqi army met the defence commander Kong Xuan (孔宣). Jiang Ziya noticed that five colored beam was emitted from Kong Xuan's back, indicating that Kong Xuan had the black magic power. Several Xiqi warriors were swept away by the five colored beam. In addition, the beam was capable of collecting magical weapons. Jiang Ziya tried to blow Kong Xuan with his magical whip, but Kong Xuan captured the whip by his five colored beam.

孔雀製造的麻煩

紂王派了更多人去攻擊西岐，但無人勝利返回。另一邊，姜子牙勸說武王應當主動出擊，推翻昏庸的紂王，令人們免於受苦。武王任命姜子牙為指揮官，命令西岐大軍向東征伐。

西岐軍在金雞嶺對陣商軍的守將孔宣。姜子牙發現孔宣的背後發出五色光，這表示孔宣會使用巫術。西岐的幾員大將都被五色光擒獲。除此之外，五色光還可以吸人法寶。姜子牙用打神鞭攻擊孔宣，但孔宣用五色光收走鞭子。

文法正誤句

 KEY 93

 Zhou Wang sent more men to attack Xiqi, but <u>none had returned</u> with victory.

 Zhou Wang sent more men to attack Xiqi, but <u>nothing had returned</u> with victory.

解析 代名詞 none 是 no one 的縮寫，相當於沒有人。Nothing 是指沒有物品。

🔥 *KEY 94*

On the other hand, Jiang Ziya <u>persuaded Wu Wang that they should</u> initiate attacks to overthrow the fatuous Zhou Wang and save people from suffering.

On the other hand, Jiang Ziya <u>persuaded that they should</u> initiate attacks to overthrow the fatuous Zhou Wang and save people from suffering.

中譯 姜子牙勸說武王應當主動出擊，推翻昏庸的紂王，令人們免於受苦。

解析 Persuade sb that ＋子句，表示說服某人做某事。其中 sb 做子句的主詞，不能省略。

🔥 *KEY 95*

Wu Wang <u>appointed Jiang Ziya</u> as the general commander and <u>ordered</u> the Xiqi army to head east.

Wu Wang <u>ordered Jiang Ziya</u> as the general commander and <u>appointed</u> the Xiqi army to head east.

中譯 武王任命姜子牙為指揮官，命令西岐大軍向東征伐。

解析 Appoint 是指定、任命的意思，後面要接人做受詞。Order 表示命令。兩個動詞的位置不能替換。

KEY 96

Jiang Ziya noticed that five colored <u>beam was emitted</u> from Kong Xuan's back.

Jiang Ziya noticed that five colored <u>beam was emitting</u> from Kong Xuan's back.

中譯 姜子牙發現孔宣的背後發出五色光。

解析 光線應當是被光源發出，應當是被動態。

24-2 封神榜小故事 │ 🔊 MP3 48
準提馴服了孔雀

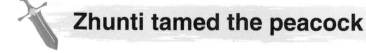

Zhunti tamed the peacock

Yang Jian borrowed the Demon Exposing Mirror (照妖鏡), hoping to detect what kind of monster Kong Xuan was; nonetheless, the mirror failed to figure out Kong

Xuan's nature. During the subsequent battles, Kong Xuan deprived Yang Jian's Howling Celestial Dog and Li Jing's pagoda. Jiang Ziya had to wave the Apricot Coloured Flag to block Kong Xuan's magical beam to prevent further loss.

After he was blocked by Kong Xuan, Wu Wang had the thought of retreating. Master Lu Ya encouraged Jiang Ziya that there must be ways to subdue Kong Xuan. Several days later, highly respected Taoist Master Zhunti (準提道人) arrived at Jiang Ziya's camp. Zhunti said he was predestined to meet Kong Xuan and guide him to the right path. Zhunti battled Kong Xuan with a twig, and revealed Kong Xuan's original shape as a giant peacock. Zhunti tamed the peacock and rode it away, rescuing everyone who had been swept up by Kong Xuan's five coloured beam.

準提馴服了孔雀

楊戩借了照妖鏡來檢查孔宣是什麼妖怪，可是照妖鏡沒有照出孔宣的原形。在後來的戰鬥中，孔宣收走了楊戩的哮天犬和李靖的寶塔。姜子牙只得用杏黃旗擋住孔宣的五色光來防止更多犧牲。

被孔宣阻擋後，武王想到要撤軍。陸壓道長鼓勵姜子牙說一定有

制服孔宣的辦法。幾天後，德高望重的準提道人來到了姜子牙的帳中。準提道人說他命中注定要遇見孔宣，並指引他走上正途。準提道人用樹枝和孔宣作戰，揭露出孔宣的原形是隻大孔雀。準提馴服了孔雀並騎著牠離開，之前被孔宣用五色光俘獲的人全數獲救。

 「文法出題要點」

（　）1. Yang Jian borrowed the Demon Exposing Mirror, hoping to _____ what kind of monster Kong Xuan was.

（A）detected　　　　（B）detecting
（C）detect　　　　　（D）to detect

答　案	D
題目中譯	楊戩借來照妖鏡來檢查孔宣是什麼妖怪。
文法重點	不定詞表示目的。
關鍵知識	動詞不定詞可以做副詞，表示目的或原因。
文法解析	楊戩借來照妖鏡是為了查明孔宣是什麼妖怪，因而不定詞是正確選項。

（　）2. _____, the mirror failed to figure out Kong Xuan's nature.

（A）Nonetheless　　　　（B）Besides

（C）Furthermore　　　　（D）While

答　案　A

題目中譯　可是照妖鏡沒有查出孔宣的原型。

文法重點　副詞連接詞的用法。

關鍵知識　Nonetheless 和 nevertheless 表示轉折，意思是但是、可是、儘管如此。nonetheless/nevertheless 是副詞，如果用在子句之間，前面須用分號。

文法解析　選項 A 是轉折含義的副詞連接詞，其餘選項則是並列或遞進的含義。

（　）3. Zhunti said he was predestined to meet Kong Xuan and ＿＿＿＿＿＿ him to the right path.

（A）guiding　　　　（B）guided

（C）guides　　　　（D）guide

答　案　D

題目中譯　準提道人說他命中注定要遇見孔宣，並指引他走上正途。

文法重點　不定詞 to 後面的動詞要用原形。

關鍵知識　如果不定詞 to 後帶有多個並列關係的動詞，動詞都應當是原形。

文法解析　這個句子中 meet 和 guide 都受到 to 的限制。

（　）4. Zhunti battled Kong Xuan with a twig, and _____ Kong Xuan's original shape as a giant peacock.

（A）invented 　　　　（B）checked

（C）realised 　　　　（D）revealed

答　　案　D

題目中譯　準提道人用樹枝和孔宣作戰，揭露出孔宣的原形是隻大孔雀。

文法重點　動詞的選用。

關鍵知識　Reveal 有披露、揭露的意思，類似的動詞還有 disclose, release 等。

文法解析　D 有揭露的含意，其餘選項都與句子意思不相關。

通天教主

分詞、時態

25-1 封神榜小故事 | MP3 49
通天教主被激怒

The Grand Master of Heaven's indignation

Jiang Ziya split his army into three parts, marching towards Sishui Pass (氾水關), Green Dragon Pass (青龍關), and Good Dream Pass (佳夢關) respectively. The general guarding Good Dream Pass was killed by the Xiqi army. To get revenge, the general's teacher Fire Spirit Goddess (火靈聖母) came to fight with Jiang Ziya. The Goddess sprinkled glaring lights and injured Jiang Ziya's arm.

Grand Completion came and saved Jiang Ziya's life. He killed the Goddess with the Heaven Revolving Seal.

Knowing the Goddess was the disciple of the Grand Master of Heaven (通天教主), Grand Completion flew to the Green Touring Palace (碧游宮) to apologise. He expressed his sincere apology and explained to the Grand Master that Jiang Ziya was authorised to penalize anyone who opposed Xiqi, as Jiang Ziya was designated to execute the mission of the heaven.

通天教主被激怒

姜子牙兵分三路，分別向汜水關、青龍關和佳夢關前進。佳夢關的守將被西岐軍所殺，引來了將軍的師父火靈聖母來報仇。火靈聖母對戰姜子牙，她灑出令人目眩的金光，並砍傷了姜子牙的手臂。

廣成子趕來救了姜子牙，他也用翻天印殺死了火靈聖母。知道了火靈聖母是通天教主的門徒，廣成子就飛去碧游宮道歉。他表達了真誠的道歉，也向通天教主解釋了姜子牙有權懲處任何對抗西岐的人，因為姜子牙已被任命為天意的執行者。

KEY 97

Jiang Ziya split his army into three parts, marching towards Sishui Pass , Green Dragon Pass , and Good Dream Pass <u>respectively</u>.

Jiang Ziya split his army into three parts, marching towards Sishui Pass , Green Dragon Pass , and Good Dream Pass <u>separately.</u>

中譯 姜子牙兵分三路,分別向氾水關、青龍關和佳夢關前進。

解析 Separately 和 respectively 意思相近,在羅列出幾個項目時常用 respectively,表示按照提及的順序逐一地⋯⋯,而 separately 更強調分離的、獨立的狀態。

KEY 98

The general guarding Good Dream Pass was killed by the Xiqi army.

The general guarded Good Dream Pass was killed by the Xiqi army.

中譯 佳夢關的守將被西岐軍所殺。

解析 分詞在放在被修飾的名詞之後作後位修飾時,現在分詞有主動含義,而過去分詞有被動含義。將軍是做出守關動作的

人，應當用現在分詞。

KEY 99

Knowing the Goddess was the disciple of the Grand Master of Heaven, Grand Completion flew to the Green Touring Palace to apologise.

Knowing the Goddess was the disciple of the Grand Master of Heaven, Grand Completion flew to the Green Touring Palace to apology.

中譯 知道了火靈聖母是通天教主的門徒，廣成子就飛去碧游宮道歉。

解析 用於不定詞中 to 後面必須接動詞。Apology 是名詞的道歉的意思，不過它的複數形式 apologies 和動詞剛好相同。

KEY 100

He expressed his sincere apology and explained to the Grand Master that Jiang Ziya was authorised to penalize anyone who opposed Xiqi.

He expressed his sincere apology and explained to the Grand Master that Jiang Ziya was authorised to penalize anyone whom opposed Xiqi.

中譯 他表達了真誠的道歉，也向通天教主解釋了姜子牙有權懲處任何對抗西岐的人。

25-2 封神榜小故事 | 🎧 *MP3 50*
懼留孫制服了申公豹

Juliusun subdued Shen Gongbao 懼留孫制服了申公豹

The Grand Master of Heaven had understood and forgiven Grand Completion. He banned everyone in Jie Sect (截教) from impeding Jiang Ziya's mission. However, Fire Spirit Goddess' fellow apprentice were unsatisfied with their teacher's decision. They plotted to take vengeance on Grand Completion. Grand Master's disciples lied to him saying that Grand Completion slandered and laughed at their Sect. The Grand Master went angry and permitted his disciples to set up the Immortal Slaughtering Formation (誅仙陣) in the Boundary Marker Pass (界碑關) to punish Jiang Ziya.

Back to Good Dream Pass, Shen Gongbao attacked Jiang Ziya with his Heavenly Ball (天珠). Juliusun subdued Shen Gongbao and imprisoned him under the Unicorn

Cliff (麒麟崖). Shen Gongbao could only beg for mercy and swear to never attack Jiang Ziya again.

懼留孫制服了申公豹

通天教主理解和寬恕了廣成子，他禁止截教門人妨礙姜子牙的使命。但是火靈聖母的同門對老師的決定很不滿，他們策劃向廣成子報仇。通天教主的徒弟們騙他說，廣成子誹謗和嘲笑截教。通天教主被激怒，允許他的弟子去界碑關擺誅仙陣，以懲戒姜子牙。

回到佳夢關，申公豹用天珠攻擊了姜子牙。懼留孫制服了申公豹，把他壓在了麒麟崖下。申公豹只得求饒，並發誓再也不會襲擊姜子牙。

「文法出題要點」

（ ）1. The Grand Master of Heaven had understood and ＿＿＿＿＿ Grand Completion.

　　（Ａ）forgiving　　　　（Ｂ）forgiven
　　（Ｃ）forgave　　　　（Ｄ）forgive

答　案　B

題目中譯　通天教主理解和寬恕了廣成子。

文法重點	動詞時態
關鍵知識	完成式為 have／has／had＋過去分詞。
文法解析	通天教主的理解和寬恕是過去完成式，動詞 forgive 也受到 had 影響，要用過去分詞 forgiven。

（ ）2. He banned everyone in Jie Sect _____ Jiang Ziya's mission.

（A）by impeding   （B）from impeding
（C）impede   （D）to impede

答　　案	B
題目中譯	他禁止截教門人妨礙姜子牙的使命。
文法重點	動詞禁止的用法。
關鍵知識	表示禁止的固定用法有 prohibit sb from doing sth／ban sb from doing sth／forbid sb to do sth
文法解析	本句用了 ban sb from doing sth，應當選 from impeding。

（ ）3. However, Fire Spirit Goddess' fellow apprentice _____ with their teacher's decision.

（A）unsatisfies　　　　（B）are unsatisfied

（C）unsatisfied　　　　（D）were unsatisfied

答　案　D

題目中譯　但是火靈聖母的同門對老師的決定很不滿。

文法重點　Be＋形容詞。

關鍵知識　動詞 satisfy 並沒有反義詞 unsatisfy，而是有相反意義的形容詞 unsatisfied。

文法解析　由於全文都是過去式，動詞應當用 were 而不是 are。Unsatisfied 是形容詞，要用 be unsatisfied。

（　）4. They plotted to take vengeance _____ Grand Completion.

（A）to　　　（B）in　　　（C）by　　　（D）on

答　案　D

題目中譯　他們策劃向廣成子報仇。

文法重點　報仇的固定搭配。

關鍵知識　To take vengeance on/upon sb for sth 表示因為某事物對某人進行報復。

文法解析　廣成子是被報仇的對象，前面介詞為 on 或 upon。

楊戩

名詞、動名詞、條件句

26-1 封神榜小故事 | MP3 51
化血神刀的解藥

The antidote of the Blood Resolving Knife

General Yu Hua at Sishui Pass once captured Huang Feihu on his defection to Xiqi. Nezha saved Huang's family and snatched Yu Hua's treasure weapon. Yu Hua returned to Penglai Mountain (蓬萊山); he practised diligently and created a powerful new weapon - the Blood Resolving Knife.

When the Xiqi army arrived at the Sishui Pass, Yu Hua requested to have a duel with Nezha and hit Nezha badly with the Blood Resolving Knife. Later, the wing of

Leizhenzi was scratched by the knife, making him faint to the ground. <u>To find out what kind of poison Yu Hua's saber possesses, Yang Jian used his Divine Skill to temporarily send away his soul,</u> and allowed Yu Hua to cut him. Yang Jian then went to the Jade Spring Mountain with the wound to consult his master Jade Tripod.

 ## 化血神刀的解藥

泡水關的將軍余化曾經俘虜過逃往西岐的黃飛虎。哪吒救了黃飛虎一家，並搶走了余化的寶物。余化回到蓬萊山後潛心修習，練成了厲害的新法寶——化血神刀。

西岐大軍來到泡水關後，余化點名和哪吒對戰，並用化血神刀重傷哪吒。之後，雷震子被化血神刀割到翅膀，昏倒在地上。為了探明余化的刀有什麼毒，楊戩用玄功暫時遁出元神，讓余化砍傷他。然後帶傷去了玉泉山向師父玉頂真人請教。

 ## 文法正誤句

 ### *KEY 101*

 General Yu Hua at Sishui Pass once captured Huang Feihu on <u>his defection</u> to Xiqi.

✗ General Yu Hua at Sishui Pass once captured Huang Feihu on his defect to Xiqi.

中譯 氾水關的將軍余化曾經俘虜過逃往西岐的黃飛虎。

解析 名詞 defection 表示背叛、叛逃到某地；defect 做名詞時表示缺點、缺陷、不足之處，做動詞才表示變節和逃跑。

KEY 102

○ Nezha saved Huang's family and snatched Yu Hua's treasure weapon.

✗ Nezha saved Huang's family and borrowed Yu Hua's treasure weapon.

中譯 哪吒救了黃飛虎一家，並搶走了余化的寶物。

解析 根據句子的意義，哪吒應當是把寶物搶走而不是借走。

KEY 103

○ He practised diligently and created a powerful new weapon - the Blood Resolving Knife.

✗ He practising diligently and creating a powerful new weapon - the Blood Resolving Knife.

中譯 他潛心修習，練成了厲害的新法寶——化血神刀。

解析 動名詞不是動詞，句子中沒有動詞是錯誤的用法。

KEY 104

To find out what kind of poison Yu Hua's saber has, Yang Jian used his Divine Skill to <u>temporarily send away his soul.</u>

To find out what kind of poison Yu Hua's saber has, Yang Jian used his Divine Skill to <u>temporary send away his soul.</u>

中譯 為了探明余化的刀有什麼毒，楊戩用玄功暫時遁出元神。

解析 副詞 temporarily 修飾動詞 send，而形容詞 temporary 不能修飾動詞。

26-2 封神榜小故事 | 🎧 MP3 52
三粒解藥

Three pills of the antidote

The Jade Tripod examined Yang Jian's wound, and identified that it was caused by the Blood Resolving Knife. People will lose their life if the wound site bleeds. The reason why Leizhenzi was able to survive was becaue his wings were made from apricots. Jade Tripod said the poison was created by Yu Yuan of the Penglai Island, who was also Yu Hua's teacher. Yu Yuan was the only person who possessed the medicine for the Blood Resolving Knife.

Yang Jian transformed himself into Yu Hua's appearance and arrived at Penglai Island. The fake Yu Hua told his teacher that he accidentally hurt himself with the knife during practice. Thus, Yang Jian obtained three pills of the antidote, and healed Nezha, Leizhenzi and himself. In the subsequent battle, Yang Jian killed Yu Hua, and the Xiqi army took over the Sishui Pass without encountering much resistance.

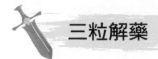 ## 三粒解藥

玉頂真人檢查了楊戩的傷口，看出刀傷是化血神刀所致。如果傷口流血人就會送命。雷震子能活下來是因為他的雙翅乃是仙杏化成。玉頂真人説毒物是蓬萊島余元所製，余元也是余化的師父。余元是化血神刀解藥的唯一擁有者。

楊戩變身成余化的樣子來到蓬萊島。假余化對余元説自己練習時失手被神刀誤傷。於是楊戩得到了三粒解藥，醫好了哪吒、雷震子和他自己。楊戩在接下來的戰役中殺死了余化。西岐軍沒有遇到更多抵抗就攻下了汜水關。

「文法出題要點」

( ) 1. The Jade Tripod examined Yang Jian's wound, and identified that it _____ the Blood Resolving Knife.

（A）by   （B）caused by
（C）was   （D）was caused by

答　案	D
題目中譯	玉頂真人檢查了楊戩的傷口，看出刀傷是化血神刀所致。
文法重點	被動語態。
關鍵知識	主詞是動作的承受者時用被動語態。
文法解析	主詞 it 指的是楊戩的刀傷，化血神刀是發出動作的物品，所以應當選擇 was caused by。

( ) 2. People will lose their life if the wound site _____.

（A）will bleed   （B）is bleeding
（C）bleeds   （D）bleed

答　　案	C
題目中譯	如果傷口流血人就會送命。
文法重點	If 條件句，假設語氣。
關鍵知識	從屬連接詞 if 連接時態不一致的主句和從句。如果 if 子句是一般現在式，if 子句應當是將來式。
文法解析	子句中如果傷口流血，bleed 應當用一般現在式，並且動詞要做第三人稱單數變化。

(　) 3. Leizhenzi survived for his wings were made _____ apricots.

(A) at
(B) by
(C) in
(D) from

答　　案	D
題目中譯	雷震子能活下來是因為他的雙翅乃是仙杏化成。
文法重點	Be made of 和 be made from。
關鍵知識	一般在製造過程中涉及化學轉變或本質上的改變的，會用 made from；其他情況下常用 made of。
文法解析	四個選項中只有 from 可以與 made 搭配。

（　）4. Jade Tripod said the poison was created by Yu Yuan of the Penglai Island, ＿＿＿＿＿＿ was also Yu Hua's teacher.

（A）whom 　　　　　　（B）that
（C）which 　　　　　　（D）who

答　　案	D
題目中譯	玉頂真人說毒物是蓬萊島余元所製，余元也是余化的師父。
文法重點	形容詞子句。
關鍵知識	關係代名詞要和先行詞相匹配。
文法解析	蓬萊島的余元雖然寫作 Yu Yuan of the Penglai Island，但是先行詞是人，要用 who 或 whom。而關係代名詞做子句的主詞，因而要用主格 who。

27-1 封神榜小故事 | MP3 53
余元殞命

The death of Yu Yuan

Yu Yuan later realized that he was cheated by Yang Jian. Then he heard that Yang Jian had killed Yu Hua. So he came to punish Yang Jian. Jiang Ziya blocked Yu Yuan with the Apricot colored Flag, and Li Jing took this chance to stab Yu Yuan's leg. Yu Yuan fled away with his camel.

Tuxingsun burrowed through the ground and reached Yu Yuan's tent. He found Yu Yuan was in meditation with his eyes closed. Tuxingsun stealthily mounted the camel. He rode the camel away , but the camel came back to Yu

Yuan at its own will. Yu Yuan grabbed Tuxingsun's head firmly and threw him into the Universal Bag (乾坤袋). Yu Yuan made a fire and planned to burn Tuxingsun to death. However, Juliusun made a storm that blew the bag away and saved Tuxingsun.

余元殞命

　　余元後來意識到自己被楊戩所騙，然後他又得知楊戩殺死了余化，就趕來教訓楊戩。姜子牙用杏黃旗擋住余元的攻擊，李靖趁機刺傷了余元的腿。余元騎著他的駱駝逃跑。

　　土行孫遁地來到余元的帳篷，他發現余元正在閉眼打坐。土行孫偷偷騎上了駱駝。他騎著駱駝跑掉，但是駱駝又自己回到了余元的身邊。余元緊緊抓住土行孫的頭，把他丟到了乾坤袋中。余元升起大火，準備燒死土行孫。不過，懼留孫施法刮起暴風，將乾坤袋吹走救了土行孫。

文法正誤句

KEY 105

Yu Yuan later realized that <u>he was cheated by Yang Jian</u>, then he heard that Yang Jian had killed Yu Hua.

Yu Yuan later realized that <u>he was cheated Yang Jian</u>, then he heard that Yang Jian had killed Yu Hua.

中譯 余元後來意識到自己被楊戩所騙，然後他又聽說楊戩殺死了余化。

解析 A is cheated by B 句型中，B 是發出動作的人，前面要有介詞 by。

KEY 106

Jiang Ziya blocked Yu Yuan with the Apricot colored Flag, <u>and Li Jing took this chance</u> to stab Yu Yuan's leg.

Jiang Ziya blocked Yu Yuan with the Apricot colored Flag, <u>and Li Jing taking this chance</u> to stab Yu Yuan's leg.

中譯 姜子牙用杏黃旗擋住余元的攻擊，李靖趁機刺傷了余元的腿。

解析 兩個並列關係的子句中，每一個子句都要有動詞，動名詞 taking 不能做句子的動詞。

KEY 107

He found Yu Yuan was in meditation <u>with his eyes closed</u>.

218

He found Yu Yuan was in meditation <u>and his eyes closed</u>.

中譯 他發現余元正在閉眼打坐。

解析 With his eyes closed 是介系詞片語表示狀態，如果改成連接詞 and，則需要改寫為 and his eyes were closed。

KEY 108

 Tuxingsun stealthily <u>mounted the camel</u>.

Tuxingsun stealthily <u>mounted to the camel</u>.

中譯 土行孫偷偷騎上了駱駝。

解析 Mount 是及物動詞，相當於 climb up，不需要介系詞。

27-2 封神榜小故事 ｜ MP3 54
余元被輾為兩半

Yu Yuan was halved

During a duel, Juliusun captured Yu Yuan with the Immortal-binding Rope. Jiang Ziya ordered capital punishment for Yu Yuan. <u>But when people tried to behead Yu Yuan, they could just add a small scratch on</u>

his neck. Jiang Ziya then locked Yu Yuan into an iron box and threw it into the sea; however, Yu Yuan managed to break through the box and returned to the Green Touring Palace, where his teacher The Grand Master of Heaven was located.

The Grand Master of Heaven became outraged after hearing Yu Yuan's complaint. He vowed to give Jiang Ziya a detrimental strike. Yu Yuan came back with more treasures and returned to battle Juliusun, but he was again captured by the Immortal-binding Rope. People still had no idea how to deal with Yu Yuan. At the time, Master Lu Ya arrived at Xiqi. Lu Ya opened the gourd lid, a white bright light as sharp as a fierce blade came out and split Yu Yuan into two halves.

 ## 余元被輾為兩半

在決鬥中，懼留孫用捆仙繩捉起了余元。姜子牙命令將余元斬首，但人們要砍余元的頭時，只會輕輕劃傷他的脖頸。姜子牙又將余元鎖在鐵箱中丟入海底，但是余元成功逃出鐵箱回到他師父通天教主所在的碧游宮。那裡有他的師父通天教主。

通天教主聽到余元的遭遇十分憤怒，他發誓要給姜子牙致命的懲

罰。余元帶著更多寶物回來挑戰懼留孫，再一次被捆仙繩俘虜。眾人還是不知道要如何處置余元。此時剛好陸壓道人趕到了西岐。陸壓取出一個葫蘆，他打開葫蘆蓋子，就有明亮的白光從葫蘆中穿透出來。光線如同鋒利的尖刀，將余元劈為兩半。

 「文法出題要點」

（　）1. But when people tried to behead Yu Yuan, they _____ just add a small scratch on his neck.

    （A）be　　　　　　（B）are
    （C）could　　　　　（D）must

答　案　C

題目中譯　但人們要砍余元的頭時，只會輕輕劃傷他的脖頸。

文法重點　情態動詞。

關鍵知識　情態動詞添加意義於主動詞上。

文法解析　只會增加一點點劃傷應當用情態動詞 could。

（　）2. Yu Yuan managed to break through the box and returned to the Green Touring Palace, _____ his teacher The Grand Master of Heaven was located.

（A）where （B）when
（C）which （D）what

（　）3. He vowed to give Jiang Ziya a _____ strike.

（A）destroy （B）ravage
（C）devastate （D）detrimental

（　）4. People still had no idea ＿＿＿＿＿＿ to deal with Yu Yuan.

(A) about how　　　　(B) of how
(C) on how　　　　　(D) how

答　　案	D
題目中譯	眾人還是不知道要如何處置余元。
文法重點	Have no idea 的用法。
關鍵知識	I have no idea 相當於 I don't know，後面直接接句子或接介系詞＋名詞。
文法解析	How to deal with Yu Yuan 是一個句子，前面不需要加介系詞。

Unit 28

四位道人

關係代名詞、情態動詞、被動語態

28-1 封神榜小故事 | 🎧 MP3 55
誅仙陣前的較量

Battle against the Immortal Slaughtering Formation

The Xiqi army moved forward to the Boundary Marker Pass, but they were intercepted by the Immortal Slaughtering Formation. Jiang Ziya had to invite many Taoist Priests to discuss the strategy of breaking the formation. Almost all the immortals from the Chan Sect had arrived, including Yellow Dragon Immortal (黃龍真人), Burning Lamp, Master of the Clouds, Taiyi Immortal, Pure Essence, Juliusun, Master Lu Ya, Jade Tripod, Grand Completion, etc. No one dared enter the dangerous formation. They waited patiently for the arrival of Primeval

Lord of Heaven.

The Immortal Slaughtering Formation was designed by the Grand Master of Heaven and set up by his disciples in the Jie Sect. The formation had four gates; it required four immortals to break them separately. After Primeval Lord of Heaven arrived, he invited three other prominent Taoist priests Taishang Laojun (太上老君), Master Zhunti, and Master Jieyin (接引道人) to jointly destroy the Immortal Slaughtering Formation.

 ## 誅仙陣前的較量

　　西岐大軍前進到界碑關，被誅仙陣擋住去路。姜子牙只好延請許多道長來商討破陣的方法。闡教的所有法師幾乎都來了，包括黃龍真人、燃燈道人、雲中子、太乙真人、赤精子、懼留孫、陸壓道人、玉頂真人、廣成子等。沒有人敢進到危險的陣中，大家都耐心等候元始天尊的到來。

　　誅仙陣由通天教主設計，截教門人所建。誅仙陣有四座大門，需要四位神仙分別破解。元始天尊駕臨後，就請來了三位重要的道教長老：太上老君、準提道人和接引道人來合作破解誅仙陣。

文法正誤句

KEY 109

○ The Xiqi army moved forward to <u>the Boundary Marker Pass, but</u> they were intercepted by the Immortal Slaughtering Formation.

✗ The Xiqi army moved forward to <u>the Boundary Marker Pass, so</u> they were intercepted by the Immortal Slaughtering Formation.

中譯 西岐大軍前進到界碑關，但被誅仙陣擋住去路。

解析 依句意要選 but，表示但是被誅仙陣擋住去路。

KEY 110

○ Jiang Ziya <u>had to invite</u> many Taoist Priests to discuss the strategy of breaking the formation.

✗ Jiang Ziya <u>had to invited</u> many Taoist Priests to discuss the strategy of breaking the formation.

中譯 姜子牙只好延請許多道長來商討破陣的方法。

解析 片語 have to 表達必須去做，to 後面接原形動詞。

KEY 111

No one <u>dared enter</u> the dangerous formation.

No one <u>dared entering</u> the dangerous formation.

中譯 沒有人敢進到危險的陣中。

解析 Dare 用作實義動詞時，後面接動詞不定詞，其中 to 可以省略，即 dare (to) do。Dare 用作情態動詞時，後面接原形動詞。Dare 後面不能接動名詞。

KEY 112

The Immortal Slaughtering Formation was <u>designed</u> by the the Grand Master of Heaven <u>and</u> <u>set up</u> by his disciples in the Jie Sect.

The Immortal Slaughtering Formation was <u>designed</u> by the the Grand Master of Heaven <u>and</u> <u>sets up</u> by his disciples in the Jie Sect.

中譯 誅仙陣由通天教主設計，截教門人所建。

解析 Set up 前面省略了動詞 was，set 是過去分詞表示被動。

Pulled down the Immortal Slaughtering Formation 摧毀誅仙陣

Primeval Lord of Heaven told everyone that four priests including himself would break the formation. After entering, swords on the gates flew towards the four masters. Masters wielded formidable power. They wrecked all the gates and pulled down the Immortal Slaughtering Formation.

Grand Master of Heaven was surrounded by the four masters after the cracking down of the formation. However, the Grand Master of Heaven was unwilling to surrender. He sneaked to the Purple Ganoderma Cliff (紫芝崖) and built an altar there. Grand Master of Heaven set up a Six Spirits Streamer (六魂幡), which had six names written on it, including the four masters, Jiang Ziya, and Wu Wang. He planned to use black magic to curse them all to death.

摧毀誅仙陣

　　元始天尊告訴大家說：包括他在內的四位道長要來破陣。在進陣後，門上的寶劍就飛向四位道長。但是四位大師施展出強大的功力，他們破壞了所有大門並摧毀了誅仙陣。

　　誅仙陣被破解後，通天教主被四位道人包圍。但是通天教主不願意投降，他逃到紫芝崖設立了一座神壇，豎起來六魂幡。幡上寫了四位道人、姜子牙和武王的名字，準備作法害死六人。

「文法出題要點」

（　）1. Primeval Lord of Heaven told everyone that four priests including himself _____ break the formation.

　　　（A）can　　　　　　（B）will
　　　（C）could　　　　　（D）would

答　　案	C
題目中譯	原始天尊告訴大家說：包括他在內的四位道長要來破陣。
文法重點	情態動詞
關鍵知識	整個句子是過去式，因而情態動詞也要用過去式。
文法解析	元始天尊告訴大家他們將要去破陣，因而動詞選擇

will。因為元始天尊所說的話受到動詞 told 的限制，情態動詞也要用過去式 would。

（　）2. After _____, swords on the gates flew towards the four masters.

（A）enter （B）entering
（C）enters （D）entered

答　案　B

題目中譯　在他們進陣後，門上的寶劍就飛向四位道長。

文法重點　After＋動詞 ing。

關鍵知識　After 後面如果沒有名詞而直接接動詞，要把動詞改成動名詞形式。

文法解析　After 之後不能直接接原形動詞。

（　）3. Grand Master of Heaven was _____ by the four masters after the cracking down of the formation.

（A）surrounds （B）surround
（C）surrounded （D）surrounding

答　　案	C
題目中譯	誅仙陣被破解後，通天教主被四位道人包圍。
文法重點	被動語態
關鍵知識	被包圍是被動語態 be surrounded。
文法解析	動詞 was 後面應當接過去分詞，而非原形動詞或動名詞。

（　）4. He sneaked to the Purple Ganoderma Cliff and built ＿＿＿＿＿＿ altar there.

　　　　（A）that　　　　　　　（B）the
　　　　（C）a　　　　　　　　（D）an

答　　案	D
題目中譯	他逃到紫芝崖設立了一座神壇。
文法重點	不定冠詞的用法。
關鍵知識	沒有特定指代的情況應當用不定冠詞 a，a 後的字第一個音為母音時，a 要改為 an。
文法解析	神壇並沒有特定的指代，所以用不定冠詞。名詞 altar 是的第一個音節是母音，不定冠詞用 an。

Unit 29

姜子牙

時態、關係代名詞、慣用語

29-1 封神榜小故事 | MP3 57
姜子牙連破三關

Jiang Ziya broke through three Passes

Zhou Wang felt anxious after hearing the breaking down of Sishui Pass. He gathered all his ministers to discuss effective military strategies to block the Xiqi army. Senior Grand Tutor Qizi suggested Zhou Wang focus on the enemy and cease all his entertainments. But Zhou Wang felt reluctant to change his lifestyle.

The cracking down of the Immortal Slaughtering Formation had left the Boundary Marker Pass unprotected. Xu Gai (徐蓋), the commander in Boundary Marker Pass, requested reinforcements from Zhou Wang.

However, Daji convinced Zhou Wang that Xu Gai only plotted to drain more treasuries. Zhou Wang refused the request and killed the messenger. Xu Gai felt extremely disappointed, so he surrendered to Xiqi.

姜子牙連破三關

姜子牙大軍攻破汜水關的消息令紂王感到擔心。他召集群臣商量阻擋西岐軍的策略。太師箕子建議紂王應當停止玩樂，專心對付商朝的敵人。不過紂王不情願改變自己的生活方式。

誅仙陣被破使得界碑關沒有了屏障。界碑關守將徐蓋請求紂王增兵。但是妲己令紂王相信徐蓋只是為了騙取軍餉。紂王拒絕了增兵的請求，並殺掉了信使。徐蓋極為失望，於是向西岐投降。

文法正誤句

KEY 113

 Zhou Wang felt anxious after hearing the breaking down of Sishui Pass.

 Zhou Wang felt anxious after heard the breaking down of Sishui Pass.

中譯 姜子牙大軍攻破汜水關的消息令紂王感到擔心。

如果要用動詞的過去式 heard，句子應當變成 after he heard the news。After 後面沒有跟名詞／代名詞的情況下，要用動名詞 hearing。

KEY 114

Senior Grand Tutor <u>Qizi persuaded Zhou Wang to</u> focus on the enemy and cease all his entertainments.

Senior Grand Tutor <u>Qizi suggested Zhou Wang to</u> focus on the enemy and cease all his entertainments.

中譯 太師箕子建議紂王應當停止玩樂，專心對付商朝的敵人。

解析 動詞 persuade 後面既可以接不定詞，也可以接 that 子句。而 suggest 是一個強制性動詞，只能用主詞 +suggest+that 子句。

KEY 115

The cracking down of the Immortal Slaughtering Formation <u>had left</u> the Boundary Marker Pass unprotected.

The cracking down of the Immortal Slaughtering Formation <u>had leaving</u> the Boundary Marker Pass unprotected.

中譯 誅仙陣被破使得界碑關沒有了屏障。

解析 過去完成式是 had＋過去分詞，不可以用動名詞。

KEY 116

○ Xu Gai, the commander in Boundary Marker Pass, requested Zhou Wang for reinforcements.

✗ Xu Gai the commander in Boundary Marker Pass requested Zhou Wang for reinforcements.

中譯 界碑關守將徐蓋請求紂王增兵。

解析 界碑關守將是主詞徐蓋的同位語，同位語前後都應有逗點隔開。

29-2 封神榜小故事｜ 🎵 MP3 58
神焰扇毀瘟癀陣

Magic Flare Fan (神焰扇) destroyed a Pestilence Trap (瘟癀陣)

When Jiang Ziya led the army to Cloud Penetrating Pass (穿雲關), Lu Yue who once spread plague in Xiqi had returned to support the Shang defender. Back to the Nine Dragon Island, Lu Yue devoted himself to black magic practice and experienced massive improvement. At Cloud Penetrating Pass, Lu Yue built a Pestilence Trap (瘟　陣). He invited Jiang Ziya to enter the trap and imprisoned Jiang Ziya.

Daode Zhenjun sent his disciple Yang Ren (楊任) to save Jiang Ziya. Yang Ren brought the Magic Flare Fan (神焰扇) to the Pestilence Trap. He made a fire and burnt the trap down. Lu Yue was also burnt to death in his own trap. After recovery, Jiang Ziya led the Xiqi army to conquer Cloud Penetrating Pass.

 ## 神焰扇毀瘟癀陣

姜子牙率軍進攻至穿雲關時，之前造成西岐瘟疫的呂岳又來支持商朝的守軍。在九龍島上，呂岳潛心修練巫術，功力又增進了不少。在穿雲關，呂岳設下了瘟癀陣，他邀請姜子牙入陣並把姜子牙困在其中。

道德真君派弟子楊任來救姜子牙。楊任帶著神焰扇進入了瘟癀陣，他點起大火燒毀了瘟癀陣。呂岳也被燒死在自己設的陣中。姜子牙康復後便率軍攻陷了穿雲關。

「文法出題要點」

（　）1. Lu Yue _____ once spread plague in Xiqi had returned to support the Shang defender.

（A）whom　　　　　　（B）who

（C）which　　　　　　（D）that

答　案	B
題目中譯	之前造成西岐瘟疫的呂岳又來支持商朝的守軍。
文法重點	關係代名詞。
關鍵知識	形容詞子句的先行詞為一個人，關係代名詞要用 who 或 whom。
文法解析	在子句中，關係代名詞 who 是子句的主詞，因此要用主格。

（　）2. Lu Yue devoted to black magic _____ and experienced massive improvement.

（A）practices　　　　　（B）practises

（C）practise　　　　　（D）practice

答　案	D

題目中譯	呂岳潛心修練巫術，功力又進階不少。
文法重點	練習 practise 的動詞和名詞。
關鍵知識	Practise 是動詞而 practice 是名詞，二者意義相同。
文法解析	獻身與巫術修煉，此處需要用到 practice 名詞形式，而 practice 為不可數名詞，不需要加 s。

( ) 3. He invited Jiang Ziya to enter the trap and
_____ Jiang Ziya.

(A) prison (B) prisoned
(C) imprisoned (D) imprison

答　　案	C
題目中譯	他邀請姜子牙入陣並把姜子牙困在其中。
文法重點	關押，囚禁的用法。
關鍵知識	Prison 是名詞監獄的意思，imprison 是及物動詞關押，可以用作 to be imprisoned for sth/ doing sth。
文法解析	把姜子牙關在陣中應當用動詞 imprison 的過去式 imprisoned。

（　）4. Jiang Ziya led the Xiqi army _____Cloud Penetrating Pass.

（A）conquers　　　　　（B）conquered

（C）conquering　　　　（D）to conquer

答　　案	D
題目中譯	姜子牙率軍攻陷了穿雲關。
文法重點	動詞 lead 的用法。
關鍵知識	Lead 的兩個固定用法是 lead sb to do sth 和 lead sb into doing sth。
文法解析	這裡選用的是 lead sb to do sth，如果用動名詞，前面需要加上介系詞 into。

Unit 30

元始天尊

慣用語、動詞

30-1 封神榜小故事 | MP3 59
破萬仙陣

Cracking down the Ten Thousand Immortal Formation

On their way to the Shang capital, Jiang Ziya and his people met The Thousand Immortal Formation. This formation was also created by the Grand Master of Heaven. He had upgraded the Immortal Slaughtering Formation into an even complex level. Once again, people dared not approach the formation. Jiang Ziya sent an urgent message to Primeval Lord of Heaven, waiting for his aids to solve this new problem.

Taishang Laojun, Immortal of the South Pole, and

Master Zhunti came along with Primeval Lord of Heaven. All the immortals in Chan Sect also gathered again. Grand Master of Heaven and his disciples arrived as well. Pure Essence started the first battle with Black Cloud Fairy (烏雲仙), with the help of Master Zhunti, Pure Essence disclosed Fairy Black Cloud (烏雲仙) as a turtle. Immortal of the South Pole casted magical spells and revealed Dragon Head Fairy (虬首仙) as a Lion.

 ## 破萬仙陣

在前進商朝都城的路上，姜子牙一行人遇到了萬仙陣。萬仙陣也是出通天教主設計的。他把誅仙陣升級到更為複雜的程度。人們又一次不敢輕易接近萬仙陣，姜子牙發向元始天尊發出緊急求助，等他來幫忙破解新的問題。

太上老君、南極仙翁和準提道人陪著元始天尊一起駕臨，闡教的眾仙人也悉數到來。通天教主也帶著他的門徒出現。首戰是赤精子對陣烏雲仙，在準提道人的幫助下，赤精子讓烏雲仙現出原形，變成了一隻鰲；南極仙翁念咒使虬首仙現出獅子模樣。

 文法正誤句

KEY 117

On their way to the Shang capital, <u>Jiang Ziya and his people</u> met The Thousand Immortal Formation.

On their way to the Shang capital, <u>Jiang Ziya and his peoples</u> met The Thousand Immortal Formation.

中譯 在前進商朝都城的路上，姜子牙一行人遇到了萬仙陣。

解析 People 單純表示人時是一個不可數名詞，表示數個民族、人種時 people 是可數名詞，後面要加 s。

KEY 118

<u>Once again,</u> people dared not approach the formation.

<u>Once</u>, people dared not approach the formation.

中譯 人們又一次不敢輕易接近萬仙陣。

解析 Once again 是固定片語搭配，表示再一次、又一次，也可以用 once more 代替。Once 自身可以用做連接詞，意思是一旦⋯⋯就⋯⋯；或用作副詞，表示曾經、從前。

KEY 119

Taishang Laojun, Immortal of the South Pole, and Master Zhunti <u>came along with</u> Primeval Lord of Heaven.

Taishang Laojun, Immortal of the South Pole, and Master Zhunti <u>came alone with</u> Primeval Lord of Heaven.

中譯 太上老君、南極仙翁和準提道人陪著元始天尊一起駕臨。

解析 Come along with sb 表示隨同某人一起到來。Alone 是形容詞獨自的意思。

KEY 120

Immortal of the South Pole casted magical spells and <u>revealed</u> Dragon Head Fairy as a Lion.

Immortal of the South Pole casted magical spells and <u>was revealed</u> Dragon Head Fairy as a Lion.

中譯 南極仙翁念咒令虯首仙現出獅子模樣。

解析 南極仙翁是發出動作的人,使得虯首仙現出原形,此處應當是主動語態。

所有計劃都被粉碎了

All schemes were smashed

Spiritual Teeth Fairy (靈牙仙) tried to attack Master Universal Virtue (普賢真人), but he was locked with a chain revealing out the original elephant figure. Master Merciful Navigation turned Golden Light Fairy (金光仙) into a jaguar. Grand Master of Heaven was extremely angry because his disciples were transformed back to their primary animal figures one after another. One of his disciples Light Settle Fairy (定光仙) realized Xiqi was destined to rise. He went to the Jie Sect Immortal and revealed Grand Master of Heaven's conspiracy of the Six Spirits Streamer. Till now, all schemes made by Grand Master of Heaven were smashed. When he was on his way back to Jade Void Palace, Primeval Lord of Heaven came across Shen Gongbao who once vowed to the Lord that he would never interfere with Jiang Ziya's mission. The Lord castigated Shen Gongbao for his breach of promise. Shen Gongbao was punished to fill in the eye of the North Sea.

所有計劃都被粉碎了

　　靈牙仙試圖攻向普賢真人，卻被鎖鏈綁住現出一頭大象的原形。慈航道人將金光仙變回豹的模樣。通天教主非常生氣，但他的弟子們一個個變回了動物原形。通天教主的弟子定光仙覺悟到西岐注定會興旺，他向截教仙人們坦白了通天教主設有六魂幡的陰謀。至此通天教主的所有計劃都被粉碎了。元始天尊回到玉虛宮剛好遇到正要逃跑的申公豹，他曾對天尊立誓絕不會干擾姜子牙的使命。元始天尊斥責申公豹違背誓言，申公豹被懲罰去堵住北海海眼。

「文法出題要點」

（　）1. His disciples were transformed back to their primary animal figures one after _____ .

　　　（A）another 　　　（B）other
　　　（C）one 　　　　　（D）two

答　　案	A
題目中譯	他的弟子們一個個變回了動物原形。
文法重點	副詞片語相繼地、依次地。
關鍵知識	one after another 是固定用法，表示一個接著一個。
文法解析	一個接一個不可以說成 one after one 或 one after other。

（　）2. One of his disciples Light Settle Fariy realized Xiqi was destined to _____.

（A）rise   （B）raised

（C）raise   （D）rose

答　案　A

題目中譯　通天教主的弟子定光仙覺悟到西岐注定會興旺。

文法重點　動詞 rise 和 raise。

關鍵知識　Rise 做動詞表示上升是一個不及物動詞，過去式和過去分詞為 rose 和 risen。Raise 是及物動詞，意思是使升起來、舉起，過去式和過去分詞都是 raised。

文法解析　國運上升應當用動詞 rise，因為 rise 含義比較廣。Raise 常用在固定搭配中如：raise a subject 等等的。

（　）3. Till now, all schemes made by Grand Master of Heaven _____ smashed.

（A）are   （B）is

（C）were   （D）was

答　案　C

題目中譯　至此通天教主的所有計劃都被粉碎了。

| 文法重點 | All 引導複數名詞，動詞也用複數形式。 |

關鍵知識　All 後面接名詞時，動詞一般用複數。只有在 all 指代不可數名詞時，謂語動詞用單數，如：all of the water，all of the food 等。

文法解析　通天教主所有的詭計是一個複數名詞，要用複數動詞 were。

（　）4. The Lord castigated Shen Gongbao for his _____ of promise.

(A) disobey　　　　　　(B) disintegrate

(C) break　　　　　　　(D) breach

答　　案　D

題目中譯　元始天尊斥責申公豹違背誓言。

文法重點　違背誓言的說法。

關鍵知識　違約有很多用法，如 break a contract, violate a treaty breach, break one's promise 等等。

文法解析　這裡的「申公豹違背誓言」這件事是一個名詞，應當選擇名詞 breach。

紂王

時態、主動詞一致

31-1 封神榜小故事 | MP3 61

武王吉兆降臨，紂王末日狂歡

Wu Wang's auspicious sign and Zhou Wang's final carnival／武王吉兆降臨，紂王末日狂歡

Jiang Ziya broked the Ten Thousand Immortal Formation and conquered Lintong Pass (臨潼關) and Mianchi County (澠池縣). The Xiqi army was ready to cross the Yellow River. When Wu Wang's dragon boat reached the river center, suddenly a giant white fish jumped into the boat. Jiang Ziya congratulated the king, saying that white fish entering a boat was an auspicious sign. Wu Wang would successfully overthrow the corrupted Zhou Wang.

When Wu Wang reached the other side of the river, <u>many dukes from Shang Dynasty had been waiting for him for a long time</u>. More people had joined the Xiqi army and marched towards Chaoge (朝歌), the Shang capital.

武王吉兆降臨，紂王末日狂歡

姜子牙破萬仙陣後，又先後攻佔了臨潼關和澠池縣。西岐大軍準備渡過黃河。當武王的龍舟行至河中間時，突然一條大白魚跳上了船。姜子牙恭賀了武王，他說：白魚入船是大吉之兆，武干定會成功推翻腐敗的紂王。

武王到達河道另一邊時，許多商朝的諸侯都已經等他很久了。更多人們加入了西岐大軍，向商朝都城朝歌前進。

文法正誤句

KEY 121

○ The Xiqi army was <u>ready to cross</u> the Yellow River.

✗ The Xiqi army was <u>ready to across</u> the Yellow River.

中譯 西岐大軍準備渡過黃河。

解析 Cross 是及物動詞，是越過、渡過的意思。Across 是介系

詞，需要加上動詞描述如何穿過，如 walk across, drive across。

KEY 122

When Wu Wang's dragon boat reached the river center, suddenly a giant white fish jumped into the boat.

When Wu Wang's dragon boat reaches the river center, suddenly a giant white fish jumped into the boat.

中譯 當武王的龍舟行至河中間時，突然一條大白魚跳上了船。

解析 Reach 和 jump 兩個並列的動詞都發生在過去，要用過去式。

KEY 123

Jiang Ziya congratulated the king.

Jiang Ziya congratulated to the king.

中譯 姜子牙恭賀了武王。

解析 Congratulate 是一個及物動詞，表示祝賀、恭喜。可以說 Congratulate sb on/upon sth。

KEY 124

Many dukes from Shang Dynasty <u>had been waiting</u> for him for a long time.

Many dukes from Shang Dynasty <u>had been waited</u> for him for a long time.

中譯 許多商朝的諸侯都已經等他很久了。

解析 句子的時態是過去完成進行式，表示在武王到達對岸前，諸侯們等候他的動作已經持續進行了一段時間，且該動作在武王到達時仍持續進行中。Dukes 是發出動作的主體，had been 後要接現在分詞 waiting。

31-2 封神榜小故事 | MP3 62
對紂王失去信念

Losing faiths towards Zhou Wang

Without giving any thought to impending threat, Zhou Wang was still indulged in binge drinking with Daji. One of Daji's joys was torturing people and hearing them cry. Once she saw several people walking barefoot on ice, Daji chopped off their feet to examine why they could tolerate coldness. Another time, she dispatched people to cut several pregnant women's bellies to find out the fetus gender. <u>People in the capital harbored intense hatred to Zhou Wang and Daji.</u>

Senior Grand Tutor Qizi told Zhou Wang: <u>Jiang Ziya had led six hundred thousand soldiers to Chaoge</u>, with every day one step closer to the capital. If Zhou Wang lose the people's support, he would also lose the whole dynasty. Zhou Wang was quite angry with Qizi, so he adopted Daji's suggestion, and repelled Qizi as a slave.

紂王仍然沈迷於和妲己飲酒作樂的生活，不顧即將到來的威脅。妲己的一大愛好是折磨人並聽人哀號。有一次，她看到一些人光腳走過冰面，妲己砍掉他們的腳來檢查為什麼他們不怕冷。還有一次，她派人割開幾個孕婦的肚子，以查看胎兒性別。都城百姓都對紂王和妲己恨之入骨。

太師箕子上奏紂王說：姜子牙帶了六十萬大軍前來朝歌，每天都更接近都城。如果皇帝失盡民心，就會斷送商朝。紂王對箕子極為生氣，他採納了妲己的主意，將箕子貶為奴隸趕走。

「文法出題要點」

(　) 1. Without giving any thought to the impending danger, Zhou Wang still indulged in drinking with

Daji_____ the approaching threat.

（A）regardless of   （B）although
（C）no matter   （D）even though

答　案	A

題目中譯　紂王仍然沈迷於和妲己飲酒作樂的生活，不顧即將到來的威脅。

文法重點　不管、不論的用法。

關鍵知識　表示讓步的字有介系詞 despite, in spite of 和形容詞詞組 regardless of，三者後面都可以直接接名詞。

文法解析　Although 和 even though 也可以表示讓步和轉折，但它們都是連接詞，後面接子句。No matter 後必須有 of 才能接名詞。

（　）2. One of Daji's joys _____ torturing people and hearing them cry.

（A）were   （B）was   （C）are   （D）is

答　案	B

題目中譯　妲己的一大愛好是折磨人並聽人哀號。

文法重點　主詞動詞一致性。

關鍵知識　動詞必須在人稱與單、複數方面與主詞一致。單數主詞

需要單數動詞；複數主詞需要複數動詞。

文法解析　雖然動詞前面的名詞是複數名詞 joys，但主詞是 one of the joys，愛好之一。單數主詞的動詞應當是單數的 was。

(　) 3. People in the capital harbored intense _____ to Zhou Wang and Daji.

（A）abhor 　　　　　　（B）despise
（C）dislike 　　　　　　（D）hatred

答　案　D

題目中譯　都城百姓都對紂王和妲己恨之入骨。

文法重點　形容詞修飾名詞。

關鍵知識　形容詞可以修飾名詞，而副詞可以修飾動詞和形容詞。

文法解析　Hatred 是一個名詞，表示憎恨，可以被形容詞 intense 修飾。其餘選項都是動詞，不能用在此處。

(　) 4. Jiang Ziya had led _____ soldiers to Chaoge.

（A）six hundreds thousand
（B）six hundred thousands

（C）six hundreds thousands

（D）six hundred thousand

答　　案	D
題目中譯	姜子牙帶了六十萬大軍前來朝歌。
文法重點	數字的英文讀法。
關鍵知識	只有在前面加 several 或後面加 of 時，hundreds, thousands, million, billion 這些字才可以加 s。
文法解析	表述具體數字時，hundred 和 thousand 後都不加 s。

千里眼和順風耳
動詞、時態、關係副詞

32-1 封神榜小故事 | *MP3 63*
千里眼和順風耳

Clairvoyance and Clairaudient／千里眼和順風耳

Zhou Wang sent a notice all over the nation to recruit people fighting against Xiqi. Good incentives had attracted the brothers Gao Ming (高明) and Gao Jue (高覺) . With both of them having peculiar faces, Zhou Wang believed the brothers must be powerful warriors, so he canonised them the Brilliant Generals (神武將軍). When the brothers fought with Nezha, Gao Jue was hit by the Universal Ring, while Gao Ming was trapped by Nine Dragon Devine Fire (九龍神火). Nezha thought the brothers were eliminated, so he returned to the camp and reported victory to Jiang Ziya.

To everyone's surprise, in the following days, the Gao Brothers continuously came back to challenge Xiqi generals. No matter how many times their death had been confirmed by the generals of Jiang Ziya, they could always come back remaining unharmed. Furthermore, the brothers always knew exactly the Xiqi generals' words and behaviours, making Jiang Ziya suspect there might be spies hidden in the camp.

 千里眼和順風耳

紂王在全國發皇榜招募對抗西岐的人。重金懸賞吸引來了高明、高覺兄弟。兩兄弟面相奇異，紂王相信他們是了不起的戰士，封他們為神武將軍。高氏兄弟對陣哪吒時，高覺被乾坤圈砸到頭，而高明被九龍神火困住。哪吒以為消滅了高氏兄弟，就回營向姜子牙通報了勝利。

出乎所有人意料，在接下來的幾天，高氏兄弟都反覆前來叫陣。不論姜子牙麾下大將幾次確認了兩人已死，他們都能毫髮無傷地回來。而且兩兄弟總是清楚了解西岐眾將在軍中的言行，讓姜子牙懷疑西岐軍中出了奸細。

文法正誤句

KEY 125

⭕ Good incentives had attracted <u>the brothers Gao Ming and Gao Jue</u>.

❌ Good incentives had attracted <u>the brother Gao Ming and Gao Jue</u>.

中譯 重金懸賞吸引來了高明、高覺兄弟。

解析 兩兄弟指的是兩個人，應該用複數 brothers。

KEY 126

⭕ When the brothers fought with Nezha, Gao Jue was hit by the Universal Ring, <u>while Gao Ming</u> was trapped by Nine Dragon Devine Fire.

❌ When the brothers fought with Nezha, Gao Jue was hit by the Universal Ring, <u>but Gao Ming</u> was trapped by Nine Dragon Devine Fire.

中譯 高氏兄弟對陣哪吒時，高覺被乾坤圈砸到頭，而高明被九龍神火困住。

解析 兩兄弟分別的狀態需要用並列關係的連接詞，而非轉折關係的連接詞。

KEY 127

○ To everyone's surprise, in the following days, the Gao Brothers continuously came back to challenge Xiqi generals.

✗ To everyone surprise, in the following days, the Gao Brothers continuously came back to challenge Xiqi generals.

中譯 出乎所有人意料，在接下來的幾天，高氏兄弟都反覆前來叫陣。

解析 出乎大家的意料既可以用 to everyone's surprise，也可以用 surprise to everyone。

KEY 128

○ They could always come back remaining unharmed.

✗ They could always come back remained.

中譯 他們都能毫髮無傷的回來。

解析 remain後加形容詞作補語，其後用 unharmed 表示毫髮無傷的，為過去分詞當形容詞用。

MP3 64

Destroyed two spirits

The Gao Brothers always eavesdropped on Jiang Ziya's plans. All the military secrets in Xiqi army were leaked out. Yang Jian had no idea as to why this situation occurred, so he went to the Jade Spring Mountain to consult Jade Tripod.

Jade Tripod told Yang Jian that the two brothers were originally a peach spirit and a willow spirit in the Checkerboard Mountain. They absorbed the souls from two mud ghosts in the Xuanyuan Temple, obtaining the super power of seeing through miles away and hearing voices a long way off. Digging out the trees would destroy the two spirits.

Jiang Ziya sent Li Jing to the Checkerboard Mountain. Li Jing found the peach tree and the willow tree. He dug them out and burnt them into ashes. Leizhenzi smashed the mud ghost statues in Xuanyuan Temple. Hence, things progressed with the same relative ease after the Gao Brothers lost all their superpower.

Subjugating them was much easier.

摧毀兩精靈

　　高氏兄弟時常偷聽姜子牙的作戰計劃，西岐軍的所有機密都被洩露出去。楊戩想不通為什麼會發生此事，就趕往玉泉山向玉頂真人請教。

　　玉頂真人告訴楊戩這兩個兄弟本是棋盤山上的桃樹精和柳樹精，他們吸收了軒轅廟裡兩個泥塑鬼的靈氣，才變得能夠看千里，聽千里。把樹挖出來就能摧毀這兩個樹精。

　　姜子牙派李靖去了棋盤山。李靖找到了桃樹和柳樹，他挖出兩棵樹並把它們焚燒成灰。雷震子打破了軒轅廟內的兩座鬼差泥身。於是高氏兄弟失去了法力。征服他就容易了。

「文法出題要點」

（　　）1. All the military secrets in Xiqi army were_____.

（A）leaked in　　　　　（B）leaked
（C）leaked out　　　　（D）leaking

答　案　C

西岐軍的所有機密都被洩露。

動詞 leak 的用法。

如果是容器內氣體或液體洩露，直接用動詞 leak；如果是秘密或消息走漏，則常用短語 leak out。

Leak in 表示滲入，leak out 是消息洩露。

（　）2. Yang Jian had no idea as to ＿＿＿＿＿＿ this situation occurred.

（A）which　　　　　　（B）why
（C）what　　　　　　（D）when

答　案　B

題目中譯　楊戩想不通為什麼會發生此事。

文法重點　Figure out 的用法。

關鍵知識　Figure out 有解決、理解的意思，常與 how, why 一起用。

文法解析　所有疑問詞選項中，只有 why 符合句子的含義。

（　）3. ＿＿＿＿＿＿ out the trees would destroy the two spirits.

（A）Digging　　　　　（B）Dig

（C）Dug　　　　　　　（D）Digs

答　　案	A
題目中譯	把樹挖出來就能摧毀這兩個樹精。
文法重點	動名詞做主詞。
關鍵知識	句子的主詞是動作時，該動作中的動詞須改為動名詞。
文法解析	選項 A 之外的其他選項都是動詞，不可以直接做句子的主詞。

（　）4. Li Jing _____ the peach tree and the willow tree, he dug them out and burnt them into ashes.

（A）find　　　　　　　（B）was finding
（C）finds　　　　　　（D）found

答　　案	D
題目中譯	李靖找到了桃樹和柳樹，他挖出兩棵樹並把它們焚燒成灰。
文法重點	動詞的時態
關鍵知識	一個句子中幾個並列關係的動詞應當時態一致。
文法解析	find, dig, burn 都是過去發生的動作，都要用動詞過去式。

楊戩

慣用語、形容詞

33-1 封神榜小故事 | MP3 65
楊戩打敗梅山七怪

Yang Jian Defeated Plum Mountain Seven Monsters／楊戩打敗梅山七怪

Jiang Ziya and his people arrived in Mengjin (孟津). Jade Tripod used to warn him to be aware of the Plum Mountain Seven Monsters at Mengjin. Jiang Ziya explored who the seven monsters were. He realized that seven animals had transformed into human shape through diligent practice. The animals were: white ape, pig, buffalo, dog, goat, snake, and centipede. Of all those monsters, the white ape was the most powerful one. He adopted a human name Yuan Hong (袁洪) and took the role as the defence general of Mengjin.

Jiang Ziya sent Yang Jian to fight Zhu Zizhen (朱子真). Zhu Zizhen swallowed Yang Jian; however, Yang Jian operated superpowers in Zhu's tummy, forcing Zhu Zizhen to transform into his original form, a pig. Then Yang Xian (楊顯) came to retaliate against Yang Jian. Yang Xian showed up as a goat, bul Yang Jian transformed himself into a tiger and bit the goat.

楊戩打敗梅山七怪

姜子牙率大軍來到孟津，玉頂真人曾警告他在孟津要提防梅山七怪。姜子牙打聽了梅山七怪是誰，他發現他們是七種動物努力修煉成人形。這些動物是白猿、豬、水牛、狗、羊、蛇和蜈蚣。在七怪中白猿法術最強。他取了人名為袁洪，做了孟津的守將。

姜子牙派楊戩同朱子真作戰，朱子真將楊戩吞了下去，但楊戩在朱子真腹內作法，讓朱子真現出豬的原形。楊顯前來挑戰楊戩，楊顯現出山羊模樣，但楊戩變身為老虎猛咬山羊。

文法正誤句

KEY 129

Jade Tripod used to warn him to be aware of the Plum Mountain Seven Monsters at Mengjin.

✗ Jade Tripod used to warn him <u>to aware of</u> the Plum Mountain Seven Monsters at Mengjin.

中譯 玉頂真人曾提醒他在孟津要提防梅山七怪。

解析 形容詞 aware 意思是留意、提防，要配合動詞一起使用。

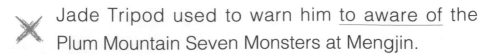

KEY 130

○ Jiang Ziya explored <u>who the seven monsters were</u>.

✗ Jiang Ziya explored <u>who were the seven monsters</u>.

中譯 姜子牙打聽了梅山七怪是誰。

解析 疑問句 who were the seven monsters 作為附屬子句要改回陳述語序。

KEY 131

○ The animals were: <u>white ape, pig, buffalo, dog, goat, snake, and centipede.</u>

✗ The animals were: <u>white ape, pig, buffalo, dog, goat, snake, centipede.</u>

中譯 這些動物是白猿、豬、水牛、狗、羊、蛇和蜈蚣。

解析 羅列一系列字時，最後一個字前面的 and 不能省略。

KEY 132

Yang Xian showed up as a goat, but Yang Jian transformed himself into a tiger and bit the goat.

Yang Xian showed up as a goat but Yang Jian transformed himself from a tiger and, but the goat.

中譯 楊顯現出山羊模樣，但楊戩變身為老虎猛咬山羊。

解析 Transform into/to 是變成某物，transform from 是從某物變成…。

33-2 封神榜小故事｜
女媧娘娘之助

MP3 66

Goddess Nuwa's help

The dog spirit Dai Li attacked Yang Jian sneakily with his concealed weapon, Howling Celestial Dog subdued Dai Li through a big fight. Yu Dasheng (余大升) the buffalo was giant in stature, Goddess Nuwa helped Yang Jian to get him under control.

Yang Jian finally fought with the mightiest Yuan Hong. Yuan Hong was a thousand-year-old ape with superb ability. Yuan Hong took Yang Jian to Plum Mountain and started fighting. Both of them wielded seventy-two transformations, but neither of them could easily prevail over the other. Yang Jian unfolded the 'Mountains and Rivers Atlas' (山河社稷圖) borrowed from Goddess Nuwa, directing Yuan Hong to walk into the picture, soon Yuan Hong found himself getting lost inside. With the atlas folded up, Yang Jian captured Yuan Hong. The ape monster was killed by Lu Ya's flying knife.

女媧娘娘之助

狗精戴禮用暗器偷襲楊戩，哮天犬藉由一場大戰制服了戴禮。水牛精余大升體量龐大，女媧娘娘協助楊戩制服了余大升。

楊戩最後對陣最強的袁洪，袁洪是能力極強的千年白猿。袁洪將楊戩引到梅山鬥法。二人各自施展出七十二變，但是兩人都無法輕易佔優勢。楊戩打開了從女媧娘娘處借來的「山河社稷圖」，將袁洪引入此圖中。袁洪很快地迷失在圖中，楊戩將圖收起來抓獲了袁洪。白猿精死於陸壓道人的飛刀之下。

「文法出題要點」

（　）1. Howling Celestial Dog _____ Dai Li through a big fight.

（A）dejected （B）victory
（C）won （D）subdued

答　　案　D

題目中譯　哮天犬通過一場大戰制服了戴禮。

文法重點　輸贏的用法。

關鍵知識　Win 做動詞表示勝過時，需要加介詞 aganist 或 over，才能接戰勝的對象。Subdue 為及物動詞，可以直接加名詞。

文法解析　只有 D 選項是前後都可以放名詞的動詞。

（　）2. Yang Jian finally fought with _____ Yuan Hong.

（A）mightiest （B）the most mighty
（C）the mightier （D）the mightiest

答　　案　D

題目中譯　楊戩最後對陣最強的袁洪。

文法重點　形容詞最高級

關鍵知識　形容詞最高級通常是在形容詞的原級後加上 est，若形容詞以 y 字母結尾，則最高級為 iest。形容詞最高級前常須加 the。

文法解析　袁洪是七怪中法術最高的，應當選擇形容詞最高級。超過三個音節的形容詞，最高級變形才是加 most，

mighty 是雙音節字，應當用一般的變形方法。

（　）3. ＿＿＿＿＿＿＿ of them could easily prevail over another.

（A）Neither   （B）Either

（C）Both   （D）None

答　案	A
題目中譯	二人都無法輕易佔優勢。
文法重點	Both, either, neither 的用法。
關鍵知識	三個字都用來談論兩者，both 意思是二者都，either 是二者中的任一，neither 是兩者皆不。如果指三個或三個以上，就需要用 all, any, none 表示三種意義。
文法解析	袁洪和楊戩是彼此無法戰勝對方，應當選 neither。

（　）4. Yang Jian ＿＿＿＿＿ the 'Mountains and Rivers Atlas' borrowed from Goddess Nuwa.

（A）unlocked   （B）opened

（C）unfolded   （D）undo

| 答　　案 | C |

題目中譯　楊戩打開了從女媧娘娘處借來的「山河社稷圖」。

文法重點　動詞打開、展開。

關鍵知識　 幾個表示打開意義的動詞中，unlock 主要強調開鎖，open 偏重於允許進入，undo 主要意思是解開，unfold 常用於展開合在一起的書或地圖。

文法解析　「山河社稷圖」類似是一種一種地圖，應當用動詞 unfold。

Unit 34

紂王

時態、限定詞、名詞子句

34-1 封神榜小故事 | MP3 67
剷除昏君

Getting Rid of the Tyrant

The Xiqi army succeeded in all the subsequent battles after cracking down Mengjin. They finally arrived at the city of Chaoge. The residents in the capital had been desperately waiting for their arrival. People congratulated each other and celebrated their emancipation. People rushed to every guarding gate and required the soldiers to let the Xiqi army in. Chaoge was smoothly liberated without any fight.

When Jiang Ziya met Zhou Wang, he proclaimed the king's ten primary crimes. All the dukes were extremely angry after hearing Zhou Wang's evil deeds, resorting to kill Zhou Wang themselves. Jiang Ziya ordered Zhou Wang to admit his crimes, but Zhou Wang refused to surrender. He fought with the dukes all by himself and got injured. He then hid himself in the Star Picking Pavilion. Daji said she would use her magic to fight Jiang Ziya.

剷除昏君

攻陷孟津後，西岐大軍取得了所有後續戰役的勝利，終於到達了朝歌。城中居民早就翹首企盼他們的到來，人們互相慶賀終於獲救了。人們衝到每個城門，要求守軍放西岐軍進入城中。朝歌城不戰而破。

姜子牙見到紂王後，細數了紂王的十大罪狀。各路諸侯聽了紂王惡行都怒不可遏，都要親手殺了昏君。姜子牙命令紂王認罪，但紂王拒絕投降。紂王獨自上陣對打各路諸侯，並且受傷。他躲進摘星樓，妲己說她要用法術挑戰姜子牙。

KEY 133

The Xiqi army succeeded in all the subsequent battles after cracking down Mengjin.

The Xiqi army was succeeded in all the subsequent battles after cracking down Mengjin.

中譯 攻陷孟津後，西岐大軍取得了所有後續戰役的勝利。

解析 Succeed 表示成功含義時，是一個主動詞。如果表示接續、接替的意思時，有可能用被動式 be succeeded。

KEY 134

The residents in the capital had been desperately waiting for their arrival.

The residents in the capital had been desperately waited for their arrival.

中譯 城中居民早就翹首企盼他們的到來。

解析 Had been waiting 為過去完成進行式，表示截至西岐軍到來前，城中居民等待他們到來的動作一直在持續。Wait 一般不用於被動態。

KEY 135

People rushed to <u>every guarding gate</u> and required the soldiers to let the Xiqi army in.

People rushed to <u>every guarding gates</u> and required the soldiers to let the Xiqi army in.

中譯 人們衝到每個城門，要求守軍放西岐軍進入城中。

解析 限定詞 every 後面的名詞要用單數。

KEY 136

Whon Jiang Ziya met Zhou Wang, he <u>proclaimed</u> the king's ten primary crimes.

When Jiang Ziya met Zhou Wang, he <u>was proclaiming</u> the king's ten primary crimes.

中譯 姜子牙見到紂王後，細數了紂王的十大罪狀。

解析 姜子牙細數罪狀是一個已經發生的事件，用一般過去式而非過去進行式。

The end of Shang Dynasty

In fact, the vixen found Zhou Wang's doom had come. With her task accomplished, <u>she decided to flee away.</u> However, Daji was intercepted and captured by Goddess Nuwa. <u>Daji argued that it was Nuwa's instruction to bewitch Zhou Wang and bring down the Shang Dynasty.</u> However, <u>Goddess Nuwa rebuked Daji for committing horrific crimes and torturing innocent people.</u> Daji was handed to Jiang Ziya.

Jiang Ziya ordered Daji to be executed for her heinous crimes, but no one was willing to kill her. Jiang Ziya brought out Lu Ya's gourd and opened the lid. A beam chopped off Daji's head and the thousand-year-old fox witch perished.

Zhou Wang asked his soldiers to gather firewood to the Star Picking Pavilion. He set a fire, and burnt himself to death. <u>The Shang Dynasty had eventually come to an end.</u>

商朝的結束

實際上，狐狸精發現紂王大限已到，她的任務已經完成，就打算逃跑。然而，妲己卻被女媧娘娘攔住並綁了起來。妲己爭辯説是女媧娘娘指示她迷惑紂王，拖垮商朝的。但女媧斥責妲己犯下可怕的罪行並折磨無辜百姓。她把妲己交給姜子牙發落。

姜子牙命令將罪惡深重的妲己處死，但是沒有人願意親手殺她。姜子牙取出陸壓道長的葫蘆，打開蓋子。一道光削去了妲己的頭，千年狐狸精就死去了。

紂王請士兵在摘星樓堆滿乾柴，點起大火，把自己燒死了。商朝終於走到了盡頭。

「文法出題要點」

（　）1. She decided to flee away as her mission _____.

　　　（A）complete　　　　（B）was completed
　　　（C）completed　　　　（D）had completed

答　　案　D
題目中譯　她的任務已經完成，就打算逃跑。
文法重點　過去完成式。

過去完成式表示過去某一動作之前已經完成了另一個動作。通常用於句子中有過去發生的兩個事件，先發生的事件用過去完成式，後發生的事件用一般過去式。

文法解析 任務完成發生於準備逃跑之前，因而用過去完成式 her mission had completed。

（　）2. Daji argued _____ it was Nuwa's instruction to bewitch Zhou Wang and bring down the Shang Dynasty.

（A）this （B）these

（C）those （D）that

答　案 D

題目中譯 妲己爭辯說是女媧娘娘指示她迷惑紂王，拖垮商朝的。

文法重點 That 引導名詞子句

關鍵知識 That 是沒有語意的從屬連接詞，that 帶領的從屬子句做為主句的受詞或補語時，可以將 that 省略。

文法解析 只有 that 可以做從屬連接詞，其他選項都是一般代詞。

（　）3. Goddess Nuwa rebuked Daji for _____ horrific crimes and torturing innocent people.

（A）committed （B）commits
（C）committing （D）commit

| 答　案 | C |

題目中譯　女媧斥責妲己犯下可怕的罪行並折磨無辜百姓。

文法重點　介系詞＋動名詞。

關鍵知識　介系詞之後只能加名詞，為了符合文法規則，動詞要變化為動名詞形式。

文法解析　C 選項之外的其他選項都不能直接接到介系詞後。

（　）4. The Shang Dynasty had eventually ＿＿＿ to the end.

（A）coming （B）comes
（C）came （D）come

| 答　案 | D |

題目中譯　商朝終於走到了盡頭。

文法重點　過去完成式。

關鍵知識　過去完成式的固定用法為 had＋過去分詞。

文法解析　Come 是不規則動詞，它的過去分詞也是 come。

Unit 35

姜子牙

被動語態、分詞

35-1 封神榜小故事 | MP3 69
姜子牙封神

Investiture of Gods

All the dukes and princes voted Wu Wang as the new king to lead the country. <u>The Zhou Dynasty was established.</u> Zhou Wang's treasures were distributed to the public. Wu Wang also amnestied all the innocent people from prison and abolished the cruel punishments of the Shang Dynasty.

Wu Wang redistributed the vassal states to launch the Zhou Dynasty officially. <u>After the completion of their mission, Yang Jian, Nezha, Leizhenzi and other immortals all left Wu Wang</u> and resumed the ascetic lives.

Jiang Ziya returned to Xiqi. Following the instruction from Primeval Lord of Heaven, he held a solemn ritual at the Investiture of Gods Platform. Jiang Ziya set up the memorial ceremony for all the generals and immortals who had sacrificed their lives during the entire battle. He read aloud the obituaries written by Primeval Lord of Heaven, and conferred altogether three hundred and sixty five deities.

 ## 姜子牙封神

所有諸侯和工了們都推舉武王為新的君主，周朝得以建立。紂王的寶物被分發給了百姓。武王也大赦了所有無辜被囚禁的人，並廢棄了商朝的殘酷刑罰。

武王重新分封諸侯，正式開啟了周王朝。使命完成後，楊戩、哪吒、雷震子和其他仙人辭別了武王，回歸清修生活。

姜子牙返回了西岐，依據元始天尊的指示，他在封神台舉辦了莊嚴的儀式。姜子牙為伐紂戰爭中所有戰死的將士和仙人舉行了紀念儀式。他宣讀了元始天尊寫的誥文，一共封了三百六十五位正神。

文法正誤句

KEY 137

○ The Zhou Dynasty <u>was established</u>.

✗ The Zhou Dynasty <u>established</u>.

中譯 周朝得以建立。

解析 Zhou Dynasty 不能主動做出動作,而是被建立,應當用被動語態。

KEY 138

○ <u>After the completion</u> of their mission, Yang Jian, Nezha, Leizhenzi and other immortals all left Wu Wang and resumed the ascetic lives.

✗ <u>After the complete</u> of their mission, Yang Jian, Nezha, Leizhenzi and other immortals all left Wu Wang and resumed the ascetic lives.

中譯 使命完成後,楊戩、哪吒、雷震子和其他仙人辭別了武王,回歸清修生活。

解析 Completion 是名詞,表示完成;complete 是形容詞或動詞,表示完整的、使……完整。

KEY 139

Jiang Ziya set up the memorial ceremony for all the generals and <u>immortals who had sacrificed</u> their lives during the entire battle.

Jiang Ziya set up the memorial ceremony for all the generals and <u>immortals whom had sacrificed</u> their lives during the entire battle.

中譯 姜子牙為伐紂戰爭中所有戰死的將士和仙人舉行了紀念儀式。

解析 形容詞子句中，關係代名詞做子句的主詞，應當用主格。

KEY 140

He read aloud <u>the obituaries written by</u> Primeval Lord of Heaven.

He read aloud <u>the obituaries writing by</u> Primeval Lord of Heaven.

中譯 他宣讀了元始天尊寫的誄文。

解析 現在分詞有主動、進行的含義，過去分詞有被動、完成的含義。誄文是被寫，選用過去分詞 written。

The god of all gods

After the investiture of gods, all deities were settled and praised. Even Shen Gongbao gained a divine title. Only one person was left over, since Jiang Ziya did not leave a title for himself. He returned all the treasure weapons to his master.

Primeval Lord of Heaven appreciated Jiang Ziya's diligent work. He allowed Jiang Ziya to retain possession of the magic whip permanently; therefore, Jiang Ziya became the god of all gods. Every deity should be subservient to Jiang Ziya. In the future, for each place that Jiang Ziya visits, the official god must temporarily abdicate in honor of Jiang Ziya. This circumstance has evolved into a common saying: all gods give way to Jiang Taigong.

 眾神之神

封神結束後，所有的神仙都得到封號和讚賞。連申公豹都獲得了一個神仙頭銜。只剩下了一個人，因為姜子牙沒有給自己封神。他將所有寶物交還給師尊。

　　元始天尊感念姜子牙的勤奮工作。他准許姜子牙永遠持有打神鞭，於是姜子牙成了眾神之神。每個神仙都要對他禮讓。今後如果姜子牙去到一處，該部正神就要暫時退位，向姜子牙表示敬意。這情況後來變成一句俗語：「太公在此，諸神迴避」。

 「文法出題要點」

（　）1. Only one person was left over, since Jiang Ziya did not _____ a title for himself.

　　（A）lcft　　　　　　　（B）leaving
　　（C）leave　　　　　　（D）leaves

答　　案　　C

題目中譯　　只剩下了一個人，因為姜子牙沒有給自己封神。

文法重點　　助動詞＋原形動詞。

關鍵知識　　助動詞 do/dose/did 一般用於否定句和疑問句，助動詞後面加動詞原形。

文法解析　　動詞 leave 表示留下，它的過去式和過去分詞是 left。在 did not 後應當是原形 leave。

（　）2. Primeval Lord of Heaven _____ Jiang Ziya's diligent work.

（A）gratitude （B）grateful

（C）thankful （D）appreciated

答　案　D

題目中譯　原始天尊感念姜子牙的勤奮工作。

文法重點　動詞感謝。

關鍵知識　表示感謝有許多搭配形容詞關鍵字的短語，如 be grateful, be thankful for, be obliged for。

文法解析　句子需要一個動詞表示感謝，只能選擇 D 選項。

（　）3. He allowed Jiang Ziya to retain possession of the magic whip permanently; _____, Jiang Ziya became the god of all gods.

（A）nevertheless （B）moreover

（C）therefore （D）however

答　案　C

題目中譯　他准許姜子牙永遠持有打神鞭，於是姜子牙成了眾神之神。

文法重點　副詞連接詞。

關鍵知識　副詞連接詞是兼有副詞作用的連接詞，它用來連接合句中的兩個對等子句。

文法解析　Therefore 為因果關係連接詞，是正確選項。其他連接詞都是表示遞進或轉折關係。

（　）4. In the future, for each place that Jiang ziya _____ the offical god must temporarily abdicate in honor of Jiang Ziya.

　　　　（A）visited　　　　　　（B）visiting

　　　　（C）will visit　　　　　（D）visits

答　案　D

題目中譯　今後如果姜子牙去到一處，該部正神就要暫時退位，向姜子牙表示敬意。

文法重點　條件句。

關鍵知識　If 條件句的主從時態不一致，if 子句是一般現在式時，主句用一般將來時。

文法解析　姜子牙訪問某地是條件子句，應當用一般現在式。主詞為第三人稱單數，動詞 visit 要加 s。

Learn Smart! 063

文法封神榜 (附 MP3)

作　　　者	武董
發 行 人	周瑞德
執行總監	齊心瑀
企劃編輯	陳韋佑
校　　　對	編輯部
封面構成	高鍾琪

內頁構成	菩薩蠻數位文化有限公司
印　　　製	大亞彩色印刷製版股份有限公司
初　　　版	2016 年 9 月
定　　　價	新台幣 369 元
出　　　版	倍斯特出版事業有限公司
電　　　話	(02) 2351-2007
傳　　　真	(02) 2351-0887
地　　　址	100 台北市中正區福州街 1 號 10 樓之 2
E - m a i l	best.books.service@gmail.com
網　　　址	www.bestbookstw.com

港澳地區總經銷	泛華發行代理有限公司
地　　　址	香港新界將軍澳工業邨駿昌街 7 號 2 樓
電　　　話	(852) 2798-2323
傳　　　真	(852) 2796-5471

國家圖書館出版品預行編目資料

文法封神榜 / 武董著. -- 初版. -- 臺
北市 : 倍斯特, 2016.09 面 ; 公分.
-- (Learn　smart! ; 63)ISBN
978-986-92855-7-5(平裝附光碟片)
1.英語 2.語法
　805.16　　　　　　105014314